The Datchet Diamonds by Richard Marsh

Richard Bernard Heldmann was born on 12th October 1857, in St Johns Wood, North London.

By his early 20's Heldmann began publishing fiction for the myriad magazine publications that had sprung up and were eager for good well-written content.

In October 1882, Heldmann was promoted to co-editor of Union Jack, a popular magazine, but his association with the publication ended suddenly in June 1883. It appears Heldman was prone to issuing forged cheques to finance his lifestyle. In April 1884 He was sentenced to 18 months hard labour.

In order to be well away from the scandal and damage this had caused to his reputation Heldmann adopted a pseudonym on his release from jail. Shortly thereafter the name 'Richard Marsh' began to appear in the literary periodicals. The use of his mother's maiden name as part of it seems both a release and a lifeline.

A stroke of very good fortune arrived with his novel The Beetle published in 1897. This would turn out to be his greatest commercial success and added some much-needed gravitas to his literary reputation.

Marsh was a prolific writer and wrote almost 80 volumes of fiction as well as many short stories, across many genres from horror and crime to romance and humour.

Index of Contents

CHAPTER I

TWO MEN AND A MAID

The band struck up a waltz. It chanced to be the one which they had last danced together at the Dome. How well he had danced, and how guilty she had felt! Conscious of what almost amounted to a sense of impropriety! Charlie had taken her; it was Charlie who had made her go—but then, in some eyes, Miss Wentworth might not have been regarded as the most unimpeachable of chaperons. That Cyril, for instance, would have had strong opinions of his own upon that point, Miss Strong was well aware.

While Miss Strong listened, thinking of the last time she had heard that waltz, the man with whom she had danced it stood, all at once, in front of her. She had half expected that it would be so—half had feared it. It was not the first time they had encountered each other on the pier; Miss Strong had already begun to more than suspect that the chance of encountering her was the magnet which drew Mr. Lawrence through the turnstiles. She did not wish to meet him; she assured herself that she did not wish to meet him. But, on the other hand, she did not wish to go out of her way so as to seem to run away from him.

The acquaintance had begun on the top of the Devil's Dyke in the middle of a shower of rain. Miss Strong, feeling in want of occupation, and, to speak the truth, a little in the blues, had gone, on an unpromising afternoon in April, on the spur of the moment, and in something like a temper, on a solitary excursion to the Devil's Dyke. On the Downs the wind blew great guns. She could hardly stand against it. Yet it did her good, for it suited her mood. She struggled on over the slopes, past Poynings, when, suddenly—she, in her abstraction, having paid no heed to the weather, and expecting nothing of the kind it came down a perfect deluge of rain. She had a walking-stick, but neither mackintosh nor umbrella. There seemed every likelihood of her having to return like a drowned rat to Brighton, when, with the appropriateness of a fairy tale, some one came rushing to her with an umbrella in his hand. She could hardly refuse the proffered shelter, and the consequence was that the owner of the umbrella escorted her first to the hotel, then to the station, and afterwards to Brighton. Nor, after such services had been rendered, when they parted at the station did she think it necessary to inform him that, not under any circumstances, was he to notice her again; besides, from what she had seen of him, she rather liked the man. So, when, two days afterwards, he stopped her on the pier to ask if she had suffered any ill-effects from her exposure, it took her some five-and-twenty minutes to explain that she had not. There were other meetings, mostly on the pier; and then, as a climax, that Masonic Ball at the Dome. She danced with him five times! She felt all the time that she ought not; she knew that she would not have done it if Cyril had been there. Miss Wentworth, introduced by Miss Strong, danced with him twice, and when asked by Miss Strong if she thought that she—Miss Strong—ought to have three dances with him Miss Wentworth declared that she did not see why, if she liked, she should not have thirty. So Miss Strong had five—which shows that Miss Wentworth's notions of the duties of a chaperon were vague.

And now the band was striking up that identical waltz; and there was Mr. Lawrence standing in front of the lady with whom he had danced it.

"I believe that that was ours, Miss Strong," he said.

"I think it was."

He was holding her hand in his, and looking at her with something in his eyes which there and then she told herself would never do. They threaded their way through the crowd of people towards the head of the pier, saying little, which was worse than saying much. Although Charlie had been working, Miss Strong wished she had stayed at home with her; it would have been better than this. A sense of pending peril made her positively nervous; she wanted to get away from her companion, and yet for the moment she did not see her way to do it.

Beyond doubt Mr. Lawrence was not a man in whose favour nothing could be said. He was of medium height, had a good figure, and held himself well. He was very fair, with a slight moustache, and a mouth which was firm and resolute. His eyes were blue—a light, bright blue—beautiful eyes they were, but scarcely of the kind which could correctly be described as sympathetic. His complexion was almost like a girl's, it was so pink and white; he seemed the picture of health. His manners were peculiarly gentle. He moved noiselessly, without any appearance of exertion. His voice, though soft, was of so penetrating a quality and so completely under control that, without betraying by any movement of his lips the fact that he was speaking, he could make his faintest whisper audible in a way which was quite uncanny. Whatever his dress might be, on him it always seemed unobtrusive; indeed, the strangest thing about the man was that, while he always seemed to be the most retiring of human beings, in reality he was one of the most difficult to be rid of, as Miss Strong was finding now. More than once, just as she was about to give him his dismissal, he managed to prevent her doing so in a manner which, while she found it impossible to resent it, was not by any means to her taste. Finally, finding it difficult to be rid of him in any other way, and being, for some reason which she would herself have found it difficult to put into words, unusually anxious to be freed from his companionship, she resolved, in desperation, to leave the pier. She acquainted him with her determination to be off, and then, immediately afterwards, not a little to her surprise and a good deal to her disgust, she found herself walking towards the pier-gates with him at her side. Miss Strong's wish had been to part from him there and then; but again he had managed to prevent the actual expression of her wish, and it seemed plain that she was still to be saddled with his society, at any rate, as far as the gates.

Before they had gone half-way down the pier Miss Strong had cause to regret that she had not shown a trifle more firmness, for she saw advancing towards her a figure which, at the instant, she almost felt that she knew too well. It was Cyril Paxton. The worst of it was that she was not clear in her own mind as to what it would be best for her to do—the relations between herself and Mr. Paxton were of so curious a character. She saw that Mr. Paxton's recognition of her had not been so rapid as hers had been of him; at first she thought that she was going to pass him unperceived. In that case she would go a few steps farther with Mr. Lawrence, dismiss him, return, and discover herself to Cyril at her leisure. But it was not to be. Mr. Paxton, glancing about him from side to side of the pier, observed her on a sudden—and he observed Mr. Lawrence too; on which trivial accident hinges the whole of this strange history.

Miss Strong knew that she was seen. She saw that Mr. Paxton was coming to her. Her heart began to beat. In another second or two he was standing in front of her with uplifted hat, wearing a not very promising expression of countenance.

"Where's Charlie?" was his greeting.

The lady was aware that the question in itself conveyed a reproach, though she endeavoured to feign innocence.

"Charlie's at home; I couldn't induce her to come out. Her 'copy' for Fashion has to be ready by the morning; she says she's behind, so she stayed at home to finish it."

"Oh!"

That was all that Mr. Paxton said, but the look with which he favoured Mr. Lawrence conveyed a very vivid note of interrogation.

"Cyril," explained Miss Strong, "this is Mr. Lawrence. Mr. Lawrence, this is Mr. Paxton; and I am afraid you must excuse me."

Mr. Lawrence did excuse her. She and Mr Paxton returned together up the pier; he, directly Mr. Lawrence was out of hearing, putting to her the question which, though she dreaded, she knew was inevitable.

"Who's that?"

"That is Mr. Lawrence."

"Yes, you told me so much already; who is Mr. Lawrence?"

As she walked Miss Strong, looking down, tapped with the ferrule of her umbrella on the boards.

"Oh! he's a sort of acquaintance."

"You have not been long in Brighton, then, without making acquaintance?"

"Cyril! I have been here more than a month. Surely a girl can make an acquaintance in that time?"

"It depends, I fancy, on the girl, and on the circumstances in which she is placed. What is Mr. Lawrence?"

"I have not the faintest notion. I have a sort of general idea that, like yourself, he is something in the City. It seems to me that nowadays most men are."

"Who introduced him?"

"A shower of rain."

"An excellent guarantor of the man's eligibility, though, even for the average girl, one would scarcely have supposed that that would have been a sufficient introduction."

Miss Strong flushed.

"You have no right to talk to me like that. I did not know that you were coming to Brighton, or I would have met you at the station."

"I knew that I should meet you on the pier."

The lady stood still.

"What do you mean by that?"

The gentleman, confronting her, returned her glance for glance.

"I mean what I say. I knew that I should meet you on the pier—and I have."

The lady walked on again; whatever she might think of Mr. Paxton's inference, his actual statement was undeniable.

"You don't seem in the best of tempera, Cyril. How is Mr. Franklyn?"

"He was all right when I saw him last—a good deal better than I was or than I am."

"What is the matter with you? Are you ill?"

"Matter!" Mr. Paxton's tone was bitter. "What is likely to be the matter with the man who, after having had the luck which I have been having lately, to crown it all finds the woman he loves philandering with a stranger—the acquaintance of a shower of rain—on Brighton pier."

"You have no right to speak to me like that—not the slightest! I am perfectly free to do as I please, as you are. And, without condescending to dispute your inferences—though, as you very well know, they are quite unjust!—any attempt at criticism on your part will be resented by me in a manner which you may find unpleasant."

A pause followed the lady's words, which the gentleman did not seem altogether to relish.

"Still the fact remains that I do love you better than anything else in the world."

"Surely if that were so, Cyril, at this time of day you and I would not be situated as we are."

"By which you mean?"

"If you felt for me what you are always protesting that you feel, surely sometimes you would have done as I wished."

"Which being interpreted is equivalent to saying that I should have put my money into Goschens, and entered an office at a salary of a pound a week."

"If you had done so you would at any rate still have your money, and also, possibly, the prospect of a career."

They had reached the end of the pier, and were leaning over the side, looking towards the Worthing lights. Miss Strong's words were followed by an interval of silence. When the gentleman spoke again, in his voice there was the suspicion of a tremor.

"Daisy, don't be hard on me."

"I don't wish to be hard. It was you who began by being hard on me."

He seemed to pay no heed to her speech, continuing on a line of his own—

"Especially just now!"

She glanced at him.

"Why especially just now?"

"Well—" He stopped. The tremor in his voice became more pronounced. "Because I'm going for the gloves."

If the light had been clearer he might have seen that her face assumed a sudden tinge of pallor.

"What do you mean by you're going for the gloves?"

"I mean that probably by this time tomorrow I shall have either won you or lost you for ever."

"Cyril!" There was a catching in her breath. "I hope you are going to do nothing—wild."

"It depends upon the point of view." He turned to her with sudden passion. "I'm sick of things as they are—sick to death! I've made up my mind to know either the best or the worst."

"How do you propose to arrive at that state of knowledge?"

"I've gone a bull on Eries—a big bull. So big a bull that if they fall one I'm done."

"How done?"

"I shall be done, because it will be for reasons, good, strong, solid reasons, the last deal I shall ever make on the London Stock Exchange."

There was silence. Then she spoke again—

"You will lose. You always do lose!"

"Thanks."

"It will be almost better for you that you should lose. I am beginning to believe, Cyril, that you never will do any good till you have touched bottom, till you have lost all that you possibly can lose."

"Thank you, again."

She drew herself up, drawing herself away from the railing against which she had been leaning. She gave a gesture which was suggestive of weariness.

"I too am tired. This uncertainty is more than I can stand; you are so unstable, Cyril. Your ideas and mine on some points are wide apart. It seems to me that if a girl is worth winning, she is worth working for. As a profession for a man, I don't think that what you call 'punting' on the Stock Exchange is much better than pitch-and-toss."

"Well?"

The word was an interrogation. She had paused.

"It appears to me that the girl who marries a man who does nothing else but 'punt' is preparing for herself a long line of disappointments. Think how many times you have disappointed me. Think of the fortunes you were to have made. Think, Cyril, of the Trumpit Gold Mine—what great things were to come of that!"

"I am quite aware that I did invest every penny I could beg, borrow, or steal in the Trumpit Gold Mine, and that at present I am the fortunate possessor of a trunkful of shares which are not worth a shilling a-piece. The reminder is a pleasant one. Proceed—you seem wound up to go."

Her voice assumed a new touch of sharpness.

"The long and the short of it is, Cyril—it is better that we should understand each other!—if your present speculation turns out as disastrously as all your others have done, and it leaves you worse off than ever, the relations, such as they are, which exist between us must cease. We must be as strangers!"

"Which means that you don't care for me the value of a brass-headed pin."

"It means nothing of the kind, as you are well aware. It simply means that I decline to link my life with a man who appears incapable of keeping his own head above water. Because he insists on drowning himself, why should I allow him to drown me too?"

"I observe that you take the commercial, up-to-date view of marriage."

"What view do you take? Are you nearer to being able to marry me than ever you were? Are you not farther off? You have no regular income—and how many entanglements? What do you propose that we should live on—on the hundred and twenty pounds a year which mother left me?"

There came a considerable silence. He had not moved from the position he had taken up against the railing, and still looked across the waveless sea towards the glimmering lights of Worthing. When he did speak his tones were cold, and clear, and measured—perhaps the coldness was assumed to hide a warmer something underneath.

"Your methods are a little rough, but perhaps they are none the worse on that account. As you say so shall it be. Win or lose, to-morrow evening I will meet you again upon the pier—that is, if you will come."

"You know I'll come!"

"If I lose it will be to say goodbye. Next week I emigrate."

She was still, so he went on—

"Now, if you don't mind, I'll see you to the end of the pier, and say goodbye until tomorrow. I'll get something to eat and hurry back to town."

"Won't you come and see Charlie?"

"Thank you, I don't think I will. Miss Wentworth has not a sufficiently good opinion of me to care if I do or don't. Make her my excuses."

Another pause. Then she said, in a tone which was hardly above a whisper—

"Cyril, I do hope you'll win."

He stood, and turned, and faced her.

"Do you really mean that, Daisy?"

"You know that I do."

"Then, if you really hope that I shall win—the double event!—as an earnest of your hopes—there is no one looking!—kiss me."

She did as he bade her.

CHAPTER II

OVERHEARD IN THE TRAIN

It was with a feeling of grim amusement that Mr. Paxton bought himself a first-class ticket. It was, probably, the last occasion on which he would ride first-class for some considerable time to come. The die had fallen; the game was lost—Eries had dropped more than one. Not only had he lost all he had to lose, he was a defaulter. It was out of his power to settle, he was going to emigrate instead. He had with him a Gladstone bag; it contained all his worldly possessions that he proposed to take with him on his travels. His intention was, having told Miss Strong the news, and having bidden a last farewell, to go straight from Brighton to Southampton, and thence, by the American line, to the continent on whose shores Europe dumps so many of its failures.

The train was later than are the trains which are popular with City men. It seemed almost empty at London Bridge. Mr. Paxton had a compartment to himself. He had an evening paper with him. He turned to the money article. Eries had closed a point lower even than he had supposed. It did not matter. A point lower, more or less, would make no difference to him—the difference would be to the brokers who had trusted him. Wishing to do anything but think, he looked to see what other news the paper might contain. Some sensational headlines caught his eye.

"ROBBERY OF THE DUCHESS OF DATCHET'S DIAMONDS!

"AN EXTRAORDINARY TALE."

The announcement amused him.

"After all that is the sort of line which I ought to have made my own—robbing pure and simple. It's more profitable than what Daisy says that I call 'punting.'"

He read on. The tale was told in the usual sensational style, though the telling could scarcely have been more sensational than the tale which was told. That afternoon, it appeared, an amazing robbery had taken place—amazing, first, because of the almost incredible value of what had been stolen; and, second, because of the daring fashion in which the deed had been done. In spite of the desperate nature of his own position—or, perhaps, because of it—Mr. Paxton drank in the story with avidity.

The Duchess of Datchet, the young, and, if report was true, the beautiful wife of one of England's greatest and richest noblemen, had been on a visit to the Queen at Windsor—the honoured guest of the Sovereign. As a fitting mark of the occasion, and in order to appear before Her Majesty in the splendours which so well became her, the Duchess had taken with her the famous Datchet diamonds. As all the world knows the Dukes of Datchet have been collectors of diamonds during, at any rate, the last two centuries.

The value of their collection is fabulous—the intrinsic value of the stones which the duchess had taken with her on that memorable journey, according to the paper, was at least £250,000—a quarter of a million of money! This was the net value—indeed, it seemed that one might almost say it was the trade value, and was quite apart from any adventitious value which they might possess, from, for instance, the point of view of historical association.

Mr. Paxton drew a long breath as he read:

"Two hundred and fifty thousand pounds—a quarter of a million! I am not at all sure that I should not have liked to have had a finger in such a pie as that. It would be better than punting at Eries."

The diamonds, it seemed, arrived all right at Windsor, and the duchess too. The visit passed off with due éclat. It was as Her Grace was returning that the deed was done, though how it was done was, as yet, a profound mystery.

"Of course," commented Mr. Paxton to himself, "all criminal London knew what she had taken with her. The betting is that they never lost sight of those diamonds from first to last; to adequately safeguard them she ought to have taken with her a regiment of soldiers."

Although she had not gone so far as a regiment of soldiers, that precaution had been taken—and precautions, moreover, which had been found to be adequate, over and over again, on previous occasions—was sufficiently plain. The duchess had travelled in a reserved saloon carriage by the five minutes past four train from Windsor to Paddington. She had been accompanied by two servants, her maid, and a man-servant named Stephen Eversleigh. Eversleigh was one of a family of servants the members of which had been in the employment of the Dukes of Datchet for generations.

It was he who was in charge of the diamonds. They were in a leather despatch-box. The duchess placed them in it with her own hand, locked the box, and retained the key in her own possession. Eversleigh carried the box from the duchess's apartment in the Castle to the carriage which conveyed her to the railway station. He placed it on the seat in front of her.

He himself sat outside with the maid. When the carriage reached the station he carried it to the duchess's saloon. The duchess was the sole occupant of the saloon. She travelled with the despatch-box in front of her all the way to London. The duke met her at Paddington. Eversleigh again placed the box on the front seat of the carriage, the duke and duchess, sitting side by side, having it in full view as the brougham passed through the London streets. The diamonds, when not in actual use, were always kept, for safe custody, at Bartlett's Bank. The confidential agent of the bank was awaiting their arrival when the brougham reached the ducal mansion in Grosvenor Square. The despatch-box was taken straight to him, and, more for form's sake than anything else, was opened by the duchess in his presence, so that he might see that it really did contain the diamonds before he gave the usual receipt.

It was as well for the bank's sake that on that occasion the form was observed. When the box was opened, it was empty! There was nothing of any sort to show that the diamonds had ever been in it— they had vanished into air!

When he had reached this point Mr. Paxton put the paper down. He laughed.

"That's a teaser. The position seems to promise a pleasing problem for one of those masters of the art of detection who have been cutting such antics lately in popular fiction. If I were appointed to ferret out the mystery, I fancy that I should begin by wanting to know a few things about her Grace the Duchess. I wonder what happened to that despatch-box while she and it were tête-à-tête? It is to be hoped that she possesses her husband's entire confidence, otherwise it is just possible that she is in for a rare old time of it."

The newspaper had little more to tell. There were the usual attempts to fill a column with a paragraph; the stereotyped statements about the clues which the police were supposed to be following up, but all that they amounted to was this: that the duchess asserted that she had placed the diamonds in the despatch-box at Windsor Castle, and that, as a matter of plain fact, they were not in it when the box reached Grosvenor Square.

Mr. Paxton leaned back in his seat, thrust his hands into his trouser pockets, and mused.

"What lucky beggars those thieves must be! What wouldn't any one do for a quarter of a million—what wouldn't I? Even supposing that the value of the stones is over-stated, and that they are only worth half as much, there is some spending in £125,000. It would set me up for life, with a little over. What prospect is there in front of me—don't I know that there is none? Existence in a country which I have not the faintest desire to go to; a life which I hate; a continual struggling and striving for the barest daily bread, with, in all human probability, failure, and a nameless grave at the end. What use is there in living out such a life as that? But if I could only lay my hands on even an appreciable fraction of that quarter of a million, with Daisy at my side—God bless the girl! how ill I have treated her!—how different it all would be!"

Mr. Paxton was possessed by a feeling of restlessness; his thoughts pricked him in his most secret places. For him, the train was moving much too slowly; had it flown on the wings of the wind it could scarcely have kept pace with the whirlwind in his brain. Rising to his feet, he began to move backwards and forwards in the space between the seats—anything was better than complete inaction.

The compartment in which he was travelling was not a new one; indeed, so far was it from being a new one, that it belonged to a type which, if not actually obsolete, at any rate nowadays is rarely seen. An oblong sheet of plate-glass was let into the partition on either side, within a few inches of the roof. This sheet of plate-glass was set in a brass frame, the frame itself being swung on a pivot.

Desirous of doing anything which would enable him, even temporarily, to escape from his thoughts, Mr. Paxton gave way to his idle and, one might almost add, impertinent curiosity. He stood, first on one seat, and peered through the glass into the adjoining compartment. So far as he was able to see, from the post of vantage which he occupied, it was vacant. He swung the glass round on its pivot. He listened. There was not a sound. Satisfied—if, that is, the knowledge gave him any satisfaction!—that there was no one there, he prepared to repeat the process of espial on the other seat.

But in this case the result was different. No sooner had he brought his eyes on a level with the sheet of glass, than he dropped down off the seat again with the rapidity of a jack-in-the-box.

"By George! I've seen that man before! It would hardly do to be caught playing the part of Peeping Tom."

Conscious of so much, he was also conscious at the same time of an increase of curiosity. Among Mr. Paxton's attributes was that one which is supposed to be the peculiar perquisite of royalty—a memory for faces. If, for any cause, a face had once been brought to his notice, he never afterwards forgot it. He had seen through that sheet of glass a countenance which he had seen before, and that quite recently.

"The chances are that I sha'n't be noticed if I am careful; and if I am caught I'll make a joke of it. I'll peep again."

He peeped again. As he did so audible words all but escaped his lips.

"The deuce! it's the beggar who was last night with Daisy on the pier."

There could not be a doubt about it; in the carriage next to his sat the individual whose companionship with Miss Strong had so annoyed him. Mr. Paxton, peering warily through the further end of the glass, treated Mr. Lawrence to a prolonged critical inspection, which was not likely to be prejudiced in that gentleman's favour.

Mr. Lawrence sat facing his observer, on Mr. Paxton's right, in the corner of the carriage. That he was not alone was plain. Mr. Paxton saw that he smiled, and that his lips were moving. Unfortunately, from Mr. Paxton's point of view, it was not easy to see who was his associate; whoever it was sat just in front of him, and therefore out of Mr. Paxton's line of vision. This was the more annoying in that Mr. Lawrence took such evident interest in the conversation he was carrying on. An idea occurred to Mr. Paxton.

"The fellow doesn't seem to see me. When I turned that other thing upon its pivot it didn't make any sound. I wonder, if I were to open this affair half an inch or so, if I could hear what the fellow's saying?"

Mr. Paxton was not in a mood to be particular. On the contrary, he was in one of those moods which come to all of us, in some dark hour of our lives, when we do the things which, being done, we never cease regretting. Mr. Paxton knelt on the cushions and he opened the frame, as he had said, just half an inch, and he put his ear as close to the opening as he conveniently could, without running the risk of being seen, and he listened. At first he heard nothing for his pains. He had not got his ear just right, and the roar of the train drowned all other sounds. Slightly shifting his position Mr. Paxton suddenly found, however, that he could hear quite well.

The speakers, to make themselves audible to each other, had to shout nearly at the top of their voices, and this, secure in their privacy, they did, the result being that Mr. Paxton could hear just as well what was being said as the person who, to all intents and purposes, was seated close beside him.

The first voice he heard was Mr. Lawrence's.

It should be noted that here and there he lost a word, as probably also did the person who was actually addressed; but the general sense of the conversation he caught quite well.

"I told you I could do it. You only want patience and resolution to take advantage of your opportunities, and a big coup is as easily carried off as a small one."

Mr. Lawrence's voice ceased. The rejoinder came from a voice which struck Mr. Paxton as being a very curious one indeed. The speaker spoke not only with a strong nasal twang, but also, occasionally, with an odd idiom. The unseen listener told himself that the speaker was probably the newest thing in races—"a German-American."

"With the assistance of a friend—eh?"

Mr. Lawrence's voice again; in it more than a suggestion of scorn.

"The assistance of a friend! When it comes to the scratch, it is on himself that a man must rely. What a friend principally does is to take the lion's share of the spoil."

"Well—why not? A man will not be able to be much of a friend to another, if, first of all, he is not a friend to himself—eh?"

Mr. Lawrence appeared to make no answer—possibly he did not relish the other's reasoning. Presently the same voice came again, as if the speaker intended to be apologetic—

"Understand me, my good friend, I do not say that what you did was not clever. No, it was damn clever!—that I do say. And I always have said that there was no one in the profession who can come near you. In your line of business, or out of it, how many are there who can touch for a quarter of a million, I want to know? Now, tell me, how did you do it—is it a secret, eh?"

If Mr. Lawrence had been piqued, the other's words seemed to have appeased him.

"Not from you—the thing was as plain as walking! The bigger the thing you have to do the more simply you do it the better it will be done."

"It does not seem as though it were simple when you read it in the papers—eh? What do you think?"

"The papers be damned! Directly you gave me the office that she was going to take them with her to Windsor, I saw how I was going to get them, and who I was going to get them from."

"Who—eh?"

"Eversleigh. Stow it—the train is stopping!"

The train was stopping. It had reached a station. The voices ceased. Mr. Paxton withdrew from his listening place with his brain in a greater whirl than ever. What had the two men been talking about? What did they mean by touching for a quarter of a million, and the reference to Windsor? The name which Mr. Lawrence had just mentioned, Eversleigh—where, quite recently, had he made its acquaintance? Mr. Paxton's glance fell on the evening paper which he had thrown on the seat. He snatched it up. Something like a key to the riddle came to him in a flash!

He opened the paper with feverish hands, turning to the account of the robbery of the Duchess of Datchet's diamonds. It was as he thought; his memory had not played him false—the person who had been in charge of the gems had been a man named Stephen Eversleigh.

Mr. Paxton's hands fell nervelessly on to his knees. He stared into vacancy. What did it mean?

The train was off again. Having heard so much, Mr. Paxton felt that he must hear more. He returned to the place of listening. For some moments, while the train was drawing clear of the station, the voices continued silent—probably before exchanging further confidences they were desirous of being certain that their privacy would remain uninterrupted. When they were heard again it seemed that the conversation was being carried on exactly at the point at which Mr. Paxton had heard it cease.

The German-American was speaking.

"Eversleigh?—that is His Grace's confidential servant—eh?"

"That's the man. I studied Mr. Eversleigh by proxy, and I found out just two things about him."

"And they were—what were they?"

"One was that he was short-sighted, and the other was that he had a pair of spectacles which the duke had given him for a birthday present, and which he thought no end of."

"That wasn't much to find out—eh?"

"You think so? Then that's where you're wrong. It's perhaps just as well for you that you don't have to play first lead."

"The treasury is more in my line—eh? However, what was the use which you made of that little find of yours?"

"If it hadn't been for that little find of mine, the possibility is that the sparklers wouldn't be where they are just now. A friend of mine had a detective camera. Those spectacles were kept in something very gorgeous in cases. My friend snapped that spectacle case with his camera. I had an almost exact duplicate made of the case from the print he got—purposely not quite exact, you know, but devilish near.

"I found myself at Windsor Station just as Her Grace was about to start for town. There were a good many people in the booking-office through which you have to pass to reach the platform. As I expected, the duchess came in front, with the maid, old Eversleigh bringing up the rear. Just as Eversleigh came into the booking-office some one touched him on the shoulder, and held out that duplicate spectacle case, saying, 'I beg your pardon, sir! Have you lost your glasses?' Of old Eversleigh's fidelity I say nothing. I don't call mere straightness anything;—but he certainly wasn't up to the kind of job he had in hand—not when he was properly handled. He has been heard to say that he would sooner lose an arm than those precious spectacles—because the duke gave them to him, you know. Perhaps he would; anyhow, he lost something worth a trifle more than his arm. When he felt himself touched on the shoulder, and saw what looked like that almighty goggle-box in the stranger's hand, he got all of a flurry, jabbed his fist into the inside pocket of his coat, and to enable him to do so popped the despatch-box down on the seat beside him—as I expected that he would do. I happened to be sitting on that seat with a rug, very nicely screened too by old Eversleigh himself, and by the stranger with the goggle-box. I nipped my rug over his box, leaving another one—own brother to the duchess's—exposed. Old Eversleigh found that the stranger's goggle-box was not his—that his own was safe in his pocket!—picked up my despatch-box, and marched off with it, while I travelled with his by the South-Western line to town; and I can only hope that he was as pleased with the exchange as I was."

The German-American's voice was heard.

"As you say, in the simplicity of your method, my good friend, was its beauty. And indeed, after all, simplicity is the very essence, the very soul, of all true art—eh?"

CHAPTER III

THE DIAMONDS

Mr. Paxton heard no more—he made no serious attempt to hear. As the German-American ceased to speak the train slowed into Preston Park. At the station Mr. Paxton saw that some one else got into the next compartment, forming a third, with its previous occupants, the rest of the way to Brighton.

Mr. Paxton had heard enough. The whirlwind in his brain, instead of becoming less, had grown more. His mental confusion had become worse confounded. He seemed unable to collect his ideas. He had attained to nothing like an adequate grasp of the situation by the time the train had arrived at its journey's end. He alighted, his Gladstone in his hand, feeling in a sort of intellectual fog. He saw Mr. Lawrence—also carrying a Gladstone—get out of the next compartment. A tall, thin man, with high cheekbones, a heavy moustache, and a pronounced stoop, got out after him—evidently the German-

American. Mr. Paxton allowed the pair to walk down the platform in front, keeping himself a respectful distance in the rear. They turned into the refreshment-room. He went in after them, taking up his position close beside them, with, however, no sort of definite intention in his head. Mr. Lawrence recognised him at once, showing that he also had a memory for faces. He nodded.

"Mr. Paxton, I believe."

Mr. Paxton admitted that that was his name, conscious, on a sudden, of a wild impulse to knock the fellow down for daring to accost him.

"What is your drink, Mr. Paxton?"

That was too much; Mr. Paxton was certainly not going to drink with the man. He responded curtly—

"I have ordered."

"That doesn't matter, does it? Drink up, and have another with me."

The fellow was actually pressing him to accept of his pestilent charity—that was how Mr. Paxton put it to himself. He said nothing—not because he had nothing to say, but because never before in his life had he felt so stupid, with so little control over either his senses or his tongue. He shook his head, walked out of the refreshment-room, got into a cab, and drove off to Makell's hotel.

Directly the cab had started and was out of the station yard he told himself that he had been a fool— doubly, trebly, a fool—a fool all round, from every possible point of view. He ought never to have let the scoundrels out of his sight; he ought to have spoken to the police; he ought to have done something; under the circumstances no one but an idiot would have done absolutely nothing at all. Never mind—for the moment it was too late. He would do something to repair his error later. He would tell Miss Strong the tale; she would rejoice to find a friend of her own figuring as the hero of such a narrative; it would be a warning to her against the making of chance acquaintance! He would ask her advice; it was a case in which two heads might be better than one.

Reaching the hotel, he went straight to his bedroom, still in a sort of mental haze. He had a wash— without, however, managing to wash much of the haze out of his head. He turned to unlock his Gladstone, intending to take out of it his brush and comb. There was something the matter with the key, or else with the lock—it would not open. It was a brand-new Gladstone, bought with a particular intent; Mr. Paxton was very far from being desirous that his proposed voyage to foreign parts should prematurely be generally known. Plainly, the lock was not in the best of order. Half abstractedly he fumbled with it for some seconds, before it could be induced to open, then it was opened rather by an exertion of force, than in response to the action of the key.

Having opened it, Mr. Paxton found himself a little puzzled by the arrangement of its contents. He could not at first remember just where he had put his brush and comb. He felt on the one side, where he had a sort of dim idea that it ought to be, and then on the other. He failed to light on it on either side. He paused for a moment to consider. Then, by degrees, distinctly remembered having placed it in a particular corner. He felt for it. It was not there. He wondered where it had contrived to conceal itself. He was certain that he had placed it in the bag. It must be in it now. He began to empty the bag of all its contents.

The first thing he took out was a shirt. He threw it from him on to the bed. As it passed through the air something fell from it on to the floor—something which came rolling against his foot. He picked it up.

It was a ring.

He could scarcely believe the evidence of his own eyes. He sat staring at the trinket in a stupor of surprise. And the more he stared the more his wonder grew. That it was a ring there could not be the slightest shadow of doubt. It was a woman's ring, a costly one—a hoop of diamonds, the stones being of unusual lustre and size.

How could such an article as that have found its way into his Gladstone bag?

He picked up another shirt, and as he did so felt that in the front there was something hard. He opened the front to see what it was. The shirt almost dropped from his hand in the shock of his amazement. Something gleamed at him from inside the linen. Taking this something out he found himself holding in his hand a magnificent tiara of diamonds.

As he knelt there, on one knee, gazing at the gaud, he would have presented a promising study for an artist possessed of a sense of humour. His mouth was open, his eyes distended to their fullest; every feature of his countenance expressed the bewilderment he felt. The presence of a ring in that brand-new bag of his was sufficiently surprising—but a tiara of diamonds! Was he the victim of some extraordinary hallucination, or the hero of a fairy tale?

He stared at the jewel, and from the jewel to the shirt, and from the shirt to the bag. Then an idea, beginning at first to glimmer on him dimly, suddenly took vivid shape, filling him with a sense of strange excitement. He doubted if the bag were his. He leant over it to examine it more closely. New brown Gladstone bags, thirty inches in length, are apt to be as like each other as peas. This was a new bag, his was a new bag—he perceived nothing in the appearance of this one to suggest that it was not his.

And yet that this was not his bag he was becoming more and more convinced. He turned to the shirt he had been holding. The contents of his bag had all been freshly purchased—obviously, this shirt had just come from the maker's too. He looked at the maker's name inside the neckband. This was not his shirt—it had been bought at a different shop; it had one buttonhole in front instead of three; it was not his size. He looked hastily at the rest of the things which were in the bag—they none of them were his. Had he had his wits about him he would have discovered that fact directly the bag was opened. Every garment seemed to have been intended to serve as cover to a piece of jewellery. He tumbled on to the bed rings, bracelets, brooches, necklets; out of vests, shirts, socks, and drawers. Till at last he stood, with an air of stupefaction, in front of a heap of glittering gems, the like of which he had scarcely thought could have existed outside a jeweller's shop.

What could be the meaning of it? By what accident approaching to the miraculous could a bag containing such a treasure trove have been exchanged for his? What eccentric and inexcusably careless individual could have been carrying about with him such a gorgeous collection in such a flimsy covering?

The key to the situation came to him as borne by a flash of lightning. They were all diamonds on the bed—nothing but diamonds. He caught up the evening paper which he had brought with him from town. He turned to the list which it contained of the diamonds which had been stolen from the Duchess of Datchet. It was as he thought. Incredible though it seemed, unless his senses played him false, in front of him were those priceless jewels—the world-famed Datchet diamonds! Reflection showed him, too, that this astounding climax had been brought about by the simplest accident. He remembered that Mr. Lawrence had alighted from the railway carriage on to the Brighton platform with the Gladstone in his hand;—he remembered now, although it had not struck him at the time, that that bag, like his own, had been brown and new. In the refreshment-room Mr. Lawrence had put his bag down upon the floor. Mr. Paxton had put his down beside it. In leaving, he must have caught up Mr. Lawrence's bag instead of his own. He had spoiled the spoiler of his spoils. Without intending to do anything of the kind, he had played on Mr. Lawrence exactly the same trick which that enterprising gentleman had himself—if Mr. Paxton could believe what he had overheard him say in the railway carriage—played on the Duchess of Datchet.

When Mr. Paxton realised exactly how it was he sat down on the side of the bed, and he trembled. It was so like a special interposition of Providence—or was it of the devil? He stared at the scintillating stones. He took them up and began to handle them. This, according to the paper, was the Amsterdam Necklace, so called because one of the Dukes of Datchet had bought all the stones for it in Amsterdam. It, alone, was worth close in the neighbourhood of a hundred thousand pounds.

A hundred thousand pounds! Mr. Paxton's fingers tingled as he thought of it. His lips went dry. What would a hundred thousand pounds not mean to him?—and he held it, literally, in the hollow of his hand. He did not know with certainty whose it was. Providence had absolutely thrown it at his head. It might not be the Duchess's, after all. At any rate, it would be but robbing the robber.

Then there was the Datchet Tiara, the Begum's Brooch, the Banee's Bracelet; if the newspaper could be credited, every piece in the collection was historical. As he toyed with them, holding them to the light, turning them this way and that, looking at them from different points of view, how the touch of the diamonds seemed to make the blood in Mr. Paxton's veins run faster!

He began to move about the bedroom restlessly, returning every now and then to take still another look at the shimmering lumps of light which were beginning to exercise over him a stronger and stronger fascination. How beautiful they were! And how low he himself had fallen! He could scarcely sink much lower. Anyhow, it would be but to pass from one ditch to another. Supposing he obtained for them even a tithe of their stated value! At this crisis in his career, what a fresh start in life five-and-twenty thousand pounds would mean! It would mean the difference between hope and helplessness, between opportunity and despair. With his experience, on such a foundation he could easily build up a monstrous fortune—a fortune which would mean happiness—Daisy's and his own. Then the five-and-twenty thousand pounds could be easily returned. Compared with what he would make with it, it was but a trifle, after all.

And then the main point was—and Mr. Paxton told himself that on that point rested the crux of the position—it would not be the Duchess of Datchet who would be despoiled; it was the robbers who, with true poetic justice, would be deprived of their ill-gotten gains. She had lost them in any case. He—he had but found them. He endeavoured to insist upon it, to himself, that he had but found them. True, there was such a thing as the finder returning what he had found—particularly when he suspected who had been the loser. But who could expect a man situated as he was to throw away a quarter of a million of money? This was not a case which could be judged by the ordinary standards of morality—it was an unparalleled experience.

Still, he could not bring himself to say, straight out, that he would stick to what he had got, and make the most of it. His mind was not sufficiently clear to enable him to arrive at any distinct decision. But he did what was almost equally fatal, he allowed himself, half unconsciously—without venturing to put it into so many words—to drift. He would see which way the wind blew, and then, if he could, go with it. For the present he would do nothing, forgetting that, in such a position as his, the mere fact of his doing nothing involved the doing of a very great deal. He looked at his watch, starting to find it was so late.

"Daisy will be tired of waiting. I must hurry, or she'll be off before I come."

He looked into the glass. Somehow there seemed to be a sort of film before his eyes which prevented him from seeing himself quite clearly, or else the light was bad! But he saw enough of himself to be aware that he was not looking altogether his usual self. He endeavoured to explain this in a fashion of his own.

"No wonder that I look worried after what I've gone through lately, and especially to-day—that sort of thing's enough to take the heart out of any man, and make him look old before his time." He set his teeth; something hard and savage came into his face. "But perhaps the luck has turned. I'd be a fool to throw a chance away if it has. I've gone in for some big things in my time; why shouldn't I go in for the biggest thing of all, and with one bold stroke more than win back all I've lost?"

He suffered his own question to remain unanswered; but he stowed the precious gems, higgledy-piggledy, inside the copy of the evening paper which contained the news of the robbery of the Duchess of Datchet's diamonds; the paper he put into a corner of the Gladstone bag which was not his; the bag he locked with greater care than he had opened it. When it was fastened, he stood for a moment, surveying it a little grimly.

"I'll leave it where it is. No one knows what there is inside it. It'll be safe enough. Anyhow, I'll give the common or garden thief a chance of providing for himself for life; his qualms on the moral aspect of the situation will be fewer than mine. If it's here when I come back I'll accept its continued presence as an omen."

He put on his hat, and he went out to find Miss Strong.

CHAPTER IV

MISS WENTWORTH'S RUDENESS

Miss Strong was growing a little tired of waiting. Indeed, she was beginning to wonder if Mr. Paxton was about to fail in still another something he had undertaken. She loitered near the gates of the pier, looking wistfully at every one who entered. The minutes went by, and yet "he cometh not," she said.

It was not the pleasantest of nights for idling by the sea. A faint, but chilly, breeze was in the air. There was a suspicion of mist. Miss Strong was growing more and more conscious that the night was raw and damp. To add to the discomfort of her position, just inside the gates of Brighton pier is not the most agreeable place for a woman to have to wait at night—she is likely to find the masculine prowler conspicuously in evidence. Miss Strong had moved away from at least the dozenth man who had accosted her, when she referred to her watch.

"I'll give him five minutes more, and then, if he doesn't come, I'm off."

Scarcely had she uttered the words than she saw Mr. Paxton coming through the turnstile. With a feeling of no inconsiderable relief she moved hastily forward. In another moment they were clasping hands.

"Cyril! I'm glad you've come at last! But how late you are!"

"Yes; I've been detained."

The moment he opened his mouth it struck her that about his manner there was something odd. But, as a wise woman in her generation, she made no comment. Together they went up the pier.

Now that he had come Mr. Paxton did not seem to be in a conversational mood. They had gone half-way up; still he evinced no inclination to speak. Miss Strong, however, excused him. She understood the cause of his silence—or thought she did. Her heart was heavy—on his account, and on her own. Her words, when they came, were intended to convey the completeness of her comprehension.

"I am so sorry."

He turned, as if her words had startled him.

"Sorry?"

"I know all about it, Cyril."

This time it was not merely a question of appearance. It was an obvious fact that he was startled. He stood stock still and stared at her. Stammering words came from his lips.

"You know all about it? What—what do you mean?"

She seemed to be surprised at his surprise. "My dear Cyril, you forget that there are papers."

"Papers?"

Still he stammered.

"Yes, papers—newspapers. I've had every edition, and of course I've seen how Eries have fallen.

"Eries? Fallen? Oh!—of course!—I see!"

She was puzzled to perceive that he appeared positively relieved, as though he had supposed and feared that she had meant something altogether different. He took off his hat to wipe his brow, although the night was very far from being unduly warm. He began walking again, speaking now glibly enough, with a not unnatural bitterness.

"They have fallen, sure enough—just as surely as if, if I had gone a bear, they would have risen. As you were good enough to say last night, it was exactly the sort of thing which might have been expected."

"I am so sorry, Cyril."

"What's the use of being sorry?"

His tone was rough, almost rude. But she excused him still.

"Is it very bad?"

Then a wild idea came to him—one which, at the moment, seemed to him almost to amount to inspiration. In the disordered condition of his faculties—for, temporarily, they were disordered—he felt, no doubt erroneously enough, that in the girl's tone there was something besides sympathy, that there was contempt as well—contempt for him as for a luckless, helpless creature who was an utter and entire failure. And he suddenly resolved to drop at least a hint that, while she was despising him as so complete a failure, even now there was, actually within his grasp, wealth sufficient to satisfy the dreams of avarice.

"I don't know what you call very bad; as regards the Eries it is about as bad as it could be. But—"

He hesitated and stopped.

"But what?" She caught sight of his face. She saw how it was working. "Cyril, is there any good news to counteract the bad? Have you had a stroke of luck?"

Yet he hesitated, already half regretting that he had said anything at all. But, having gone so far, he went farther.

"I don't want you to reckon on it just at present, but I think it possible that, very shortly, I may find myself in possession of a larger sum of money than either of us has dreamed of."

"Cyril! Do you mean it?"

Her tone of incredulity spurred him on.

"Should I be likely to say such a thing if I did not mean it? I mean exactly what I said. To be quite accurate, it is possible, nay, probable, that before very long I shall be the possessor of a quarter of a million of money. I hope that will be enough for you. It will for me."

"A quarter of a million! Two hundred and fifty thousand pounds, Cyril!"

"It sounds a nice little sum, doesn't it? I hope that it will feel as nice when it's mine!"

"But, Cyril, I don't understand. Is it a new speculation you are entering on?"

"It is a speculation—of a kind." His tone was ironical, though she did not seem to be conscious of the fact. "A peculiar kind. Its peculiarity consists in this, that, though I may not be able to lay my hands on the entire quarter of a million, I can on an appreciable portion of it whenever I choose."

"What is the nature of the speculation? Is it on the Stock Exchange?"

"That, at present, is a secret. It is not often that I have kept a secret from you; you will have to forgive me, Daisy, if I keep one now."

Something peculiar in his tone caught her ear. She glanced at him sharply.

"You are really in earnest, Cyril? You do mean that there is a reasonable prospect of your position being improved at last?"

"There is not only a reasonable prospect, there is a practical certainty."

"In spite of what you have lost in Eries?"

"In spite of everything." A ring of passion came into his voice. "Daisy, don't ask me any more questions now. Trust me! I tell you that in any case a fortune, or something very like one, is within my grasp."

He stopped, and she was silent. They went and stood where they had been standing the night before—looking towards the Worthing lights. Each seemed to be wrapped in thought. Then she said softly, in her voice a trembling—

"Cyril, I am so glad."

"I am glad that you are glad."

"And I am so sorry for what I said last night."

"What was it you said that is the particular occasion of your sorrow?"

She drew closer to his side. When she spoke it was as if, in some strange way, she was afraid.

"I am sorry that I said that if luck went against you to-day things would have to be over between us. I don't know what made me say it. I did not mean it. I thought of it all night; I have been thinking of it all day. I don't think that, whatever happens, I could ever find it in my heart to send you away."

"I assure you, lady, that I should not go unless you sent me!"

"Cyril!" She pressed his arm. Her voice sank lower. She almost whispered in his ear, while her eyes looked towards the Worthing lights. "I think that perhaps it would be better if we were to get married as soon as we can—better for both of us."

Turning, he gripped her arms with both his hands.

"Do you mean it?"

"I do; if you do the great things of which you talk or if you don't. If you don't there is my little fortune, with which we must start afresh, both of us together, either on this side of the world or on the other, whichever you may choose."

"Daisy!" His voice vibrated with sudden passion. "Will you come with me to the other side of the world in any case?"

"What—even if you make your fortune?"

"Yes; even if I make my fortune!"

She looked at him with that something on her face which is the best thing that a man can see. And tears came into her eyes. And she said to him, in the words which have been ringing down the ages—

"Whither thou goest, I will go; and where thou lodgest, I will lodge; thy people shall be my people, and thy God, my God; where thou diest, will I die, and there will I be buried; the Lord do so to me, and more also, if aught but death part thee and me!"

It may be that the words savoured to him of exaggeration; at any rate, he turned away, as if something choked his utterance. She, too, was still.

"I suppose you don't want a grand wedding."

"I want a wedding, that's all I want. I don't care what sort of a wedding it is so long as it's a wedding. And"—again her voice sank, and again she drew closer to his side—"I don't want to have to wait for it too long."

"Will you be ready to marry me within a month?"

"I will."

"Then within a month we will be married."

They were silent. His thoughts, in a dazed sort of fashion, travelled to the diamonds which were in somebody else's Gladstone bag. Her thoughts wandered through Elysian fields. It is possible that she imagined—as one is apt to do—that his thoughts were there likewise.

All at once she said something which brought him back from what seemed to be a waking dream. She felt him start.

"Come with me, and let's tell Charlie."

The suggestion was not by any means to Mr. Paxton's taste. He considered for a few seconds, seeming to hesitate. She perceived that her proposition had not been received with over-much enthusiasm.

"Surely you don't mind our telling Charlie?"

"No"—his voice was a little surly—"I don't mind."

Miss Charlotte Wentworth, better known to her intimates as Charlie, was in some respects a young woman of the day. She was thirty, and she wrote for her daily bread—wrote anything, from "Fashions" to "Poetry," from "Fiction" to "Our Family Column." She had won for herself a position of tolerable comfort, earning something over five-hundred a year with satisfactory regularity. To state that is equivalent to saying that, on her own lines, she was a woman of the world, a citizen of the New Bohemia, capable of holding something more than her own in most circumstances in which she might find herself placed, with most, if not all, of the sentiment which is supposed to be a feminine attribute knocked out of her. She was not bad-looking; dressed well, with a suggestion of masculinity; wore pince-nez, and did whatsoever it pleased her to do. Differing though they did from each other in so many respects, she and Daisy Strong had been the friends of years. When Mrs. Strong had died, and Daisy was left alone, Miss Wentworth had insisted on their setting up together, at least temporarily, a joint establishment, an arrangement from which there could be no sort of doubt that Miss Strong received pecuniary advantage. Mr. Paxton was not Miss Wentworth's lover—nor, to be frank, was she his; the consequence of which was that her brusque, outspoken method of speech conveyed to his senses—whether she intended it or not—a suggestion of scorn, being wont to touch him on just those places where he found himself least capable of resistance.

When the lovers entered, Miss Wentworth, with her person on one chair and her feet on another, was engaged in reading a magazine which had just come in. Miss Strong, desiring to avoid the preliminary skirmishing which experience had taught her was apt to take place whenever her friend and her lover met, plunged at once into the heart of the subject which was uppermost in her mind.

"I've brought you some good news—at least I think it is good news."

Miss Wentworth looked at her—a cross-examining sort of look—then at Mr. Paxton, then back at the lady.

"Good news? One always does associate good news with Mr. Paxton. The premonition becomes a kind of habit."

The gentleman thus alluded to winced. Miss Strong did not appear to altogether relish the lady's words. She burst out with the news of which she spoke, as if with the intention of preventing a retort coming from Mr. Paxton.

"We are going to be married."

Miss Wentworth displayed a possibly intentional mental opacity.

"Who is going to be married?"

"Charlie! How aggravating you are! Cyril and I, of course."

Miss Wentworth resumed her reading.

"Indeed! Well, it's no affair of mine. Of course, therefore, I should not presume to make any remark. If, however, any one should invite me to comment on the subject, I trust that I shall be at the same time informed as to what is the nature of the comment which I am invited to make."

Miss Strong went and knelt at Miss Wentworth's side, resting her elbows on that lady's knees.

"Charlie, won't you give us your congratulations?"

Miss Wentworth replied, without removing her glance from off the open page of her magazine—

"With pleasure—if you want them. Also, if you want it, I will give you eighteenpence—or even half a crown."

"Charlie! How unkind you are!"

Miss Wentworth lowered her magazine. She looked Miss Strong straight in the face. Tears were in the young lady's eyes, but Miss Wentworth showed not the slightest sign of being moved by them.

"Unfortunately, as it would seem, though I am a woman, I do occasionally allow my conduct to be regulated by the dictates of common sense. When I see another woman making a dash towards suicide I don't, as a rule, give her a helping push, merely because she happens to be my friend; preferentially, if I can, I hold her back, even though it be against her will. I have yet to learn in what respect Mr. Paxton— who, I gladly admit, is personally a most charming gentleman—is qualified to marry even a kitchen-maid. Permit me to finish. You told me last night that Mr. Paxton was going a bull on Eries; that if they fell one he would be ruined. In the course of the day they have fallen more than one; therefore, if what you told me was correct, he must be ruined pretty badly. Then, without any sort of warning, you come and inform me that you intend to marry the man who is doubly and trebly ruined, and you expect me to offer my congratulations on the event offhand! On the evidence which is at present before the court it can't be done."

"Why shouldn't I marry him, even if he is ruined?"

"Why, indeed? I am a supporter of the liberty of the female subject, if ever there was one. Why, if you wished to, shouldn't you marry a crossing-sweep? I don't know. But, on the other hand, I don't see on what grounds you could expect me to offer you my congratulations if you did."

"Cyril is not a crossing-sweep."

"No; he has not even that trade at his finger-ends."

"Charlie!" Mr. Paxton made as if to speak. Miss Strong motioned him to silence with a movement of her hand. "As it happens, you are quite wrong. It is true that Cyril lost by Eries, but he has more than made up for that loss by what he has gained in another direction. Instead of being ruined, he has made a fortune."

"Indeed! Pray, how did he manage to do that? I always did think that Mr. Paxton was a remarkable man. My confidence in him is beginning to be more than justified. And may I, at the same time, ask what is Mr. Paxton's notion of a fortune?"

"Tell her, Cyril, all about it."

Thus suffered at last to deliver his soul in words, Mr. Paxton evinced a degree of resentment which, perhaps, on the whole, was not unjustified.

"I fail to see that there is any necessity for me to justify myself in Miss Wentworth's eyes, who, on more than one occasion, has shown an amount of interest in my affairs which was only not impertinent because it happened to be feminine. But since, Daisy, you appear to be anxious that Miss Wentworth should be as satisfied on the subject of my prospects and position as you yourself are, I will do the best I can. And therefore Miss Wentworth, I would explain that my notion of a fortune is a sum equivalent to some ten or twenty times the amount you yourself are likely to be able to earn in the whole of your life."

"That ought to figure up nicely. And do you really mean to say, Mr. Paxton, that you have lost one fortune and gained another in the course of a single day?"

"I do."

"How was it done? I wish you would put me in the way of doing it for myself."

"Surely, Miss Wentworth, a woman of your capacity is qualified to do anything she pleases without prompting, and solely on her own initiative!"

"Thanks, Mr. Paxton, it's very kind of you to say such pretty things, but I am afraid you estimate my capacity a thought too highly." Miss Wentworth turned in her seat, so as to have the gentleman within her range of vision. "You understand, Mr. Paxton, very well how it is. Daisy is a lonely child. She belongs to the order of women who were in fashion before the commercial instinct became ingrained in the feminine constitution. She wants looking after. There are only Mr. Franklyn and myself to look after her. Satisfy me that, after all liabilities are settled, there is a substantial balance on the right side of your account, and I will congratulate you both."

"That, at the moment, I cannot do. But I will do this. I will undertake, in less than a fortnight, to prove myself the possessor of possibly something like a quarter of a million, and certainly of a hundred thousand pounds."

"A quarter of a million! A hundred thousand pounds! Such figures warm one's blood. One will almost begin to wonder, Mr. Paxton, if you can have come by them honestly."

The words were uttered lightly. Mr. Paxton chose to take them as if they had been meant in earnest. His cheeks flushed. His eyes flamed fire. He stood up, so beside himself with rage that it was a second or two before he could regain sufficient self-control to enable him to speak.

"Miss Wentworth, how dare you say such a thing! I have endured more from you than any man ought to endure from any woman. But when you charge me with dishonesty it is too much, even from you to me. You take advantage of your sex to address to me language for which, were the speaker a man, I would thrash him within an inch of his life."

Miss Strong, with white face, looked from one to the other.

"Cyril, she didn't mean what you think. Tell him, Charlie, that you didn't mean what he thinks."

Through her glasses Miss Wentworth surveyed the angry man with shrewd, unfaltering eyes.

"Really, Mr. Paxton puts me in a difficult position. He is so quick to take offence where none was intended, that one hardly knows what to think. Surely, when a man shows such heat and such violence in resenting what only a distorted imagination could twist into an actual imputation of dishonesty, it suggests that his own conscience can scarcely be quite clear."

Mr. Paxton seemed struggling as if to speak, and then to put a bridle on his tongue. The truth is, that he was only too conscious that he was in no mood to be a match in argument—or, for the matter of that, in retort either—for this clear-sighted lady. He felt that, if he was not careful, he would go too far; that he had better take himself away before he had made a greater exhibition of himself than he had already. So he contented himself with what was meant as an assumption of dignity.

"That is enough. Between you and me nothing more need, or can, be said. I have the honour, Miss Wentworth, of wishing you goodnight."

She showed no symptoms of being crushed. On the contrary, she retained her coolness, and also her powers of exasperation.

"Good-night, Mr. Paxton. Shall I ring the bell, Daisy, or will you show Mr. Paxton to the door?"

Miss Strong darted at her a look which, on that occasion at any rate, was not a look of love, and followed Mr. Paxton, who already had vanished from the room. Finding him in the hall, she nestled up to his side.

"I am sorry, Cyril, that this should have happened. If I had had the least suspicion of anything of the kind, I never would have asked you to come."

Mr. Paxton wore, or attempted to wear, an air of masculine superiority.

"My dear Daisy, I have seldom met Miss Wentworth without her having insulted me. On this occasion, however, she has gone too far. I will never, willingly, darken her door again. I hope you will not ask me; but if you do I shall be compelled to decline."

"It's my door as well as hers. But it won't be for long. Still, I don't think she meant what you thought she did—she couldn't be so absurd! It's a way she has of talking; she often says things without considering the construction of which they are capable."

"It is only the fact of her being a woman, my dear Daisy, which gives her the impunity of which she takes undue advantage."

"Cyril, you mustn't brand all women because of one. We are not all like that. Do you suppose that I am not aware that the person, be it man or woman, who imagines you to be capable of dishonesty either does not know you, or else is stark, raving mad? Do you think that I could love you without the absolute certainty of knowing you to be a man of blameless honour? I don't suppose you are an angel—I'm not one either, though perhaps you mightn't think it, sir! And I take it for granted that you have done plenty of things which you would rather have left undone—as I have too! But I do know that, regarded from the point of view of any standard, whether human or Divine, in all essentials you are an honest man, and that you could be nothing else."

The eulogium was a warm one—it made Mr. Paxton feel a trifle queer.

"Thank you, darling,"

So he murmured, and he kissed her.

"You will meet me again to-morrow night to tell me how the fortune fares?"

He tried to avoid doing so; but the effort only failed—he had to wince. He could only hope that she did not notice it.

"I will, my darling—on the pier."

"And mind you're punctual!"

"I promise you I'll be punctual to a second."

CHAPTER V

IN THE BODEGA

As Mr. Paxton walked away from the house in which the two ladies resided, it was with the consciousness strong upon him that his position had not been made any easier by what he had said to the lady of his love, not to speak of that lady's friend. Before he had met Miss Strong he had been, comparatively, free—free, that is, to return the diamonds to their rightful owner. Now, it seemed to him, his hands were tied—he himself had tied them. He had practically committed himself to a course of action which could only point in one direction, and that an ugly one.

"What a fool I've been!"

One is apt to tell oneself that sort of thing when the fact is already well established, and also, not only without intending to undo one's folly, but even when one actually proposes to make it more! As Mr. Paxton did then. He told himself, frankly, and with cutting scorn, what a fool he had been, and then proceeded to take what, under similar circumstances, seems to be a commonly accepted view of the situation—assuring, or endeavouring to assure himself, that to pile folly on to folly, until the height of it reached the mountain-tops, and then to undo it, would be easier than to take steps to undo it at once, while it was still comparatively a little thing.

It was perhaps this line of reasoning which induced Mr. Paxton to fancy himself in want of a drink. He turned into the Bodega. He treated himself to a whisky and soda. While he was consuming the fluid and abusing Fate, some one touched him on the shoulder. Looking round he found himself confronted by Mr. Lawrence and his friend the German-American. Not only was their appearance wholly unexpected, but obviously the surprise was not a pleasant one. Mr. Paxton clutched at the edge of the bar, glaring at the two men as if they had been ghosts.

"Good evening, Mr. Paxton."

It was Mr. Lawrence who spoke, in those quiet, level tones with which Miss Strong was familiar. To Mr. Paxton's lively imagination their very quietude seemed to convey a threat. And Mr. Lawrence kept those beautiful blue eyes of his fixed on Mr. Paxton's visage with a sustained persistence which, for some cause or other, that gentleman found himself incapable of bearing. He nodded, turned his face away, and picked up his glass.

But to do Mr. Paxton justice, he was very far from being a coward; nor, when it came to the sticking-point, was his nerve at all likely to fail him. He realised instantly that he was in a very delicate situation, and one on which, curiously enough, he had not reckoned. But if Mr. Lawrence and his friend supposed that Mr. Paxton, even if taken by surprise, was a man who could, in the long run, be taken at an advantage, they were wrong. Mr. Paxton emptied his glass, and replied to Mr. Lawrence—

"It's not a pleasant evening, is it? I think that up at the station you asked me to have a drink with you. Now, perhaps, you'll have one with me?"

As he spoke Mr. Paxton was conscious that the German-American was regarding him, if possible, even more intently than his friend. This was the man to whom he had taken an instinctive dislike. There was about the fellow a suggestion of something animal—of something almost eerie. He did not strike one as being a person with whom it would be wise to quarrel, but rather as an individual who would stick at nothing to gain his ends, and who would be moved by no appeals for either sympathy or mercy.

"Would you mind stepping outside for a moment, Mr. Paxton?"

"Outside? Why?"

Mr. Paxton's air of innocence was admirably feigned. It might be that he was a better actor with a man than with a woman.

"There is something which I rather wish to say to you."

"To me? What is it?"

"I would rather, if you don't mind, speak to you outside."

Mr. Paxton turned his back against the bar facing Mr. Lawrence with a smile.

"Aren't we private enough in here? What is it you can have to say to me?"

"You know very well what it is I have to say to you. If you take my advice, you'll come outside."

Mr. Lawrence still spoke softly, but with a softness which, if one might put it so, had in it the suggestion of a scratch. A gleam came into his eyes which was scarcely a friendly gleam. The smile on Mr. Paxton's countenance broadened.

"I know! You are mistaken. I do not know. You are the merest acquaintance; I have never exchanged half a dozen words with you. What communication of a private nature you may have to make to me, I have not the faintest notion, but, whatever it is, I would rather you said it here."

Mr. Paxton's tones were, perhaps purposely, as loud as Mr. Lawrence's were soft. What he said must have been distinctly audible, not only to those who were close to him but also to those who were at a little distance. Especially did the high words seem audible to a shabby-looking fellow who was seated at a little table just in front of them, and wore his hat a good deal over his eyes, but who, in spite of that fact, seemed to keep a very keen eye on Mr. Paxton.

Perceiving that his friend appeared to be slightly nonplussed by Mr. Paxton's manner, the German-American came a little forward, as if to his assistance. This was a really curious individual. As has been already mentioned, he was tall and thin, and, in spite of his stoop, his height was accentuated by the fashion of his attire. He wore a long, straight black overcoat, so long that it reached almost to his ankles. It was wide enough to have admitted two of him. He kept it buttoned high up to his chin. His head was surmounted by a top hat, which could scarcely have been of English manufacture, for not only was it a size or two too large for him, but, relatively, it was almost as long as his overcoat. Thus, since his hat came over his forehead, and his overcoat came up to his chin, not much of his physiognomy was visible, and what was visible was not of a kind to make one long for more. His complexion was of a dirty red. His cheekbones were high, and his cheeks were hollow. They were covered with tiny bristles, which gleamed in the light as he moved his head. His eyes were small, and black, and beady, and he had a trick of opening and shutting them, as if they were constantly being focussed. His nose was long, and thin, and aquiline—that aquiline which suggests a vulture. His voluminous moustache was black; one wondered if it owed that shade to nature. But, considerable though it was, it altogether failed to conceal his mouth, which, as the Irishman said, "rolled right round his jaws." Indeed, it was of such astonishing dimensions that the surprise which one felt on first encountering it, caused one, momentarily, to neglect to notice the practically entire absence of a chin.

This pleasing-looking person, coming to Mr. Paxton, raised a long, lean forefinger, capped by what rather resembled a talon than a human fingernail, and crooked it in Mr. Paxton's face. And he said, speaking with that pronounced German-American accent—

"Permit me, my dear friend, to ask of Mr. Paxton just one question—just one little question. Mr. Paxton, what was the colour of your Gladstone bag, eh?"

Mr. Paxton felt, as he regarded the speaker, that he was looking at what bore a stronger resemblance to some legendary evil creature than to a being of our common humanity.

"I fail to understand you, sir."

"And yet my question is a very simple one—a very simple one indeed. I ask you, what was the colour of your Gladstone bag, eh?"

"My Gladstone bag!—which Gladstone bag?"

"The Gladstone bag which you brought with you in the train from town, eh?"

Mr. Paxton gazed at his questioner with, on his countenance, an entire absence of any sort of comprehension. He turned to Mr. Lawrence—

"Is this a friend of yours?"

The pair looked at Mr. Paxton, then at each other, then back at Mr. Paxton, then again at each other. The German-American waggled his lean forefinger.

"He is very difficult, Mr. Paxton—very difficult indeed, eh? He understand nothing. It is strange. But it is like that sometimes, eh?"

Mr. Lawrence interposed.

"Look here, I'll be plain enough, even for you, Mr. Paxton. Have you got my Gladstone bag?"

Mr. Lawrence still spoke softly, but as he put his question Mr. Paxton was conscious that his eyes were fixed on him with a singular intentness, and his friend's eyes, and the eyes of the man who half concealed them with his hat, and, unless he was mistaken, the eyes of another shabby individual who was seated at a second table, between himself and the door. Indeed, he had a dim perception that sharp eyes were watching him from all over the spacious room, and that they waited for his words. Still, he managed to retain very fair control over his presence of mind.

"Your Gladstone bag! I! What the deuce do you mean?"

"What I say—have you got my Gladstone bag?"

Mr. Paxton drew himself up. Something of menace came on to his face and into his eyes. His tone became hard and dry.

"Either I still altogether fail to understand you, Mr. Lawrence, or else I understand too much. Your question is such a singular one that I must ask you to explain what construction I am intended to place upon it."

The two men regarded each other steadily, eye to eye. It is possible that Mr. Paxton read more in Mr. Lawrence's glance than Mr. Lawrence read in his, for Mr. Paxton perceived quite clearly that, in spite of the man's seeming gentleness, on the little voyage on which he was setting forth he would have to look out, at the very least, for squalls. The German-American broke the silence.

"It is that Mr. Paxton has not yet opened the Gladstone bag, and seen that a little exchange has taken place—is that so, eh?"

Mr. Paxton understood that the question was as a loophole through which he might escape. He might still rid himself of what already he dimly saw might turn out to be something worse than an Old Man of the Sea upon his shoulders. But he deliberately declined to avail himself of the proffered chance. On the contrary, by his reply he burnt his boats, and so finally cut off his escape—at any rate in that direction.

"Opened it? Of course I opened it! I opened it directly I got in. I've no more idea of what you two men are talking about than the man in the moon."

Once more the friends exchanged glances, and again Mr. Lawrence asked a question.

"Mr. Paxton, I've a particular reason for asking, and I should therefore feel obliged if you will tell me what your bag was like?"

Mr. Paxton never hesitated—he took his second fence in his stride.

"Mine? It's a black bag—rather old—with my initials on one side—stuck pretty well all over with luggage labels. But why do you ask?"

Again the two men's eyes met, Mr. Lawrence regarding the other with a glance which seemed as if it would have penetrated to his inmost soul. This time, however, Mr. Paxton's own eyes never wavered. He returned the other's look with every appearance of sang froid. Mr. Lawrence's voice continued to be soft and gentle.

"You are sure that yours was not a new brown bag?"

"Sure! Of course I'm sure! It was black; and, as for being new—well, it was seven or eight years old at least."

"Would you mind my having a look at it?"

"What do you want to have a look at it for?"

"I should esteem it a favour if you would permit me."

"Why should I?"

Again the two men's glances met. The German-American spoke.

"Where are you stopping, Mr. Paxton, eh?"

Wheeling round, Mr. Paxton treated the inquirer to anything but an enlightening answer.

"What has that to do with you? Although a perfect stranger to me—and one to whom I would rather remain a stranger—you appear to take a degree of interest in my affairs which I can only characterize as—impertinent."

"It is not meant to be impertinent, oh, dear no; oh, no, Mr Paxton, eh?"

Putting up his clawlike hand, the fellow began to rub it against his apology for a chin. Mr. Paxton turned his attention to Mr. Lawrence; it was a peculiarity of that gentleman's bearing that since his appearance on the scene he had never for a single instant removed his beautiful blue eyes from Mr. Paxton's countenance.

"You have asked me one or two curious questions, without giving me any sort of explanation; now perhaps you won't mind answering one or two for me. Have you lost a bag?"

"I can scarcely say that I have lost it. I am parted from it—for a time."

Mr. Paxton stared, as if not comprehending.

"I trust that the parting may not be longer than you appear to anticipate. Was there anything in it of value?"

"A few trifles, which I should not care to lose."

"Where, as you phrase it, did the parting take place?"

"In the refreshment-room at the Central Station—when you went out of it."

Mr. Paxton flushed—it might have been a smart bit of acting, but it was a genuine flush. He looked at the soft-toned but sufficiently incisive speaker as if he would have liked to have knocked him down; possibly, too, came very near to trying to do it. Then seemed to remember himself, confining himself instead to language which was as harsh and as haughty as he could conveniently make it.

"That is not the first time you have dropped a similar insinuation. But it shall be the last. I do not wish to have a scene in a public place, but if you address me again I will call the attention of the attendants to you, and I will have you removed."

So saying, Mr. Paxton, wheeling round on his heels, favoured the offender with a capital view of his back. To be frank, he hardly expected that his Bombastes Furioso air would prove of much effect. He had reason to think that Mr. Lawrence was not the sort of person to allow himself to be cowed by such a very unsubstantial weapon as tall-talk. His surprise was, therefore, the greater when, the words being scarcely out of his mouth, the German-American, touching his associate on the arm, made to him some sort of a sign, and without another word the two marched off together. Somewhat oddly, as it seemed, when they went out two or three other persons went out also; but Mr. Paxton particularly noticed that the man with the hat over his eyes who was seated at the little table remained behind, suddenly appearing, however, to have all his faculties absorbed in a newspaper which had been lying hitherto neglected just in front of him.

Mr. Paxton congratulated himself on the apparent effect which his words had had.

"That's a good riddance, anyhow. I don't think that I'm of the sort that's easily bluffed, but the odds were against me, and—well—the stakes are high—very high!"

As Mr. Paxton took off his hat to wipe his forehead it almost seemed that his temperature was high as well as the stakes. He called for another whisky and soda, As he sipped it, he inquired of himself how long it would be advisable for him to stop before taking his departure; he had no desire to find the enterprising associates waiting for him in the street. While he meditated some one addressed him from behind, in precisely the same words which Mr. Lawrence had originally used. Commonplace though they were, as they reached his ears they seemed to give him a sort of thrill.

"Good evening, Mr. Paxton."

Mr. Paxton turned round so quickly that some of the liquor which was in the glass that he was holding was thrown out upon the floor. The speaker proved to be a rather short and thick-set man, with a stubbly grey beard and whiskers, and a pair of shrewd, brown eyes. Mr. Paxton beheld him with as few signs of satisfaction as he had evinced on first beholding Mr. Lawrence. He tried to pass off his evident discomposure with a laugh.

"You! You're a pretty sort of fellow to startle a man like that!"

"Did I startle you?"

"When a man's dreaming of angels, he's easily startled. What's your liquid?"

"Scotch, cold. Who was that you were talking to just now?"

Mr. Paxton shot at the stranger a keen, inquisitorial glance.

"What do you mean?"

"Weren't you talking to somebody as I came in?—two men, weren't there?"

"Oh yes! One of them I never met in my life before, and I never want to meet again. The other, the younger, I was introduced to yesterday."

"The younger—what's his name?"

"Lawrence. Do you know him?"

The stranger appeared not to notice the second hurried, almost anxious look which Mr. Paxton cast in his direction.

"I fancied I did. But I don't know any one of the name of Lawrence. I must have been wrong."

Mr. Paxton applied himself to his glass. It appeared, he told himself, that he was in bad luck's way. Only one person could have been more unwelcome just at the moment than Mr. Lawrence had been, and that person had actually followed hard on Mr. Lawrence's heels. As is the way with men of his class, who frequent the highways and the byways of great cities, Mr. Paxton had a very miscellaneous acquaintance. Among them were not a few officers of police. He had rather prided himself on this fact— as men of his sort are apt to do. But now he almost wished that he had never been conscious that such a thing as a policeman existed in the world; for there—at the moment when he was least wanted— standing at his side, was one of the most famous of London detectives; a man who was high in the confidence of the dignitaries at the "Yard"; a man, too, with whom he had had one or two familiar passages, and whom he could certainly not treat with the same stand-off air with which he had treated Mr. Lawrence.

He understood now why the associates had stood not on the order of their going; it was not fear of him, as in his conceit he had supposed, which had sped their heels; it was fear of John Ireland. Gentlemen of Mr. Lawrence's kidney were pretty sure to know a man of Mr. Ireland's reputation, at any rate by sight. The "office" had been given him that a "tec." was in the neighbourhood, and Mr. Lawrence had taken himself away just in time, as he hoped, to escape recognition. That that hope was vain was obvious from what John Ireland had said. In spite of his disclaiming any knowledge of a man named Lawrence, Mr. Paxton had little doubt that both men had been "spotted."

A wild impulse came to him. He seemed to be drifting, each second, into deeper and deeper waters. Why not take advantage of what might, after all, be another rope thrown out to him by chance? Why not make a clean breast of everything to Ireland? Why not go right before it was, indeed, too late—return her diamonds to the sorrowing Duchess, and make an end of his wild dreams of fortune? No; that he would—he could not do. At least not yet. He had committed himself to Daisy, to Miss Wentworth. There was plenty of time. He could, if he chose, play the part of harlequin, and with a touch of his magic wand at any time change the scene. He even tried to flatter himself that he might play the part of an amateur detective, and track the criminals on original—and Fabian!—lines of his own; but self-flattery of that sort was too gross even for his digestion.

"Nice affair that of the Duchess of Datchet's diamonds."

The glass almost dropped from Mr. Paxton's hand. The utterance of the words at that identical instant was of course but a coincidence; but it was a coincidence of a kind which made it extremely difficult for him to retain even a vestige of self-control. Fortunately, perhaps, Mr. Ireland appeared to be unconscious of his agitation. Putting his glass down on the bar-counter, he twisted it round and round by the stem. He tried to modulate his voice into a tone of complete indifference.

"The Duchess of Datchet's diamonds? What do you mean?"

"Haven't you heard?"

Mr. Paxton hesitated. He felt that it might be just as well not to feign too much innocence in dealing with John Ireland.

"Saw something about it as I came down in the train."

"I thought you had. Came down from town?"

"Yes—just for the run."

"Came in the same train with Mr. Lawrence?"

"I rather fancy I did."

"He was in the next compartment to yours, wasn't he?"

Mr. Ireland's manner was almost ostentatiously careless, and he seemed to be entirely occupied in the contents of his glass, but for some reason Mr. Paxton was beginning to feel more and more uncomfortable.

"Was he? I wasn't aware of it. I noticed him on the platform when the train got in."

"With his friend?"

"Yes—the other man was with him."

"Went into the refreshment-room with them, didn't you, and had a drink?"

Mr. Paxton turned and looked at the speaker; Mr. Ireland seemed, as it were, to studiously refrain from looking at him.

"Upon my word, Ireland, you seem to have kept a keen eye upon my movements."

"I came down by that train too; you didn't appear to notice me."

Mr. Paxton wished—he scarcely knew why, but he did wish—that he had. He admitted that the detective had gone unrecognised, and there was a pause, broken by Mr. Ireland.

"I am inclined to think that I know where those diamonds are."

Odd how conscience—or is it the want of experience?—plays havoc with the nervous system of the amateur in crime. Ordinarily, Mr. Paxton was scarcely conscious that he had such things as nerves; he was about as cool an individual as you would be likely to meet. But since lighting on those sparkling pebbles in somebody else's Gladstone bag, he had been one mass of nerves, and of exposed nerves, too. Like some substance which is in the heart of a thunderstorm, and which is peculiarly sensitive to the propinquity of electricity, he had been receiving a continual succession of shocks. When Mr. Ireland said in that unexpected and, as Mr. Paxton felt, uncalled-for fashion that he thought that he knew where those diamonds were, Mr. Paxton was the recipient of another shock upon the spot. Half a dozen times it had been with an effort that he had just succeeded in not betraying himself; he had to make another and a similar effort then.

"You think that you know where those diamonds are?"

"I do!"

There was silence; then the officer of the law went on. Mr. Paxton wished within himself that he would not.

"You're a sporting man, Mr. Paxton. I wouldn't mind making a bet that they're not far off! There's a chance for you!"

"Oh!" It was not at all a sort of bet which Mr. Paxton was disposed to take, nor a kind of chance he relished. "Thanks; but it's a thing about which you're likely to know more than I do; I'm not betting. Are you on the job?"

"Half the Yard is on the job already."

Silence once more; then again Mr. Ireland. He stood holding his glass in his hand, twiddling it between his finger and thumb, and all his faculties seemed to be engaged in making an exhaustive examination of the liquor it contained; but Mr. Paxton almost felt as if his voice had been the voice of fate.

"The man who has those diamonds will find that they won't be of the slightest use to him. He'll find that they'll be as difficult to get rid of as the Koh-i-Nor. Like the chap who stole the Gainsborough, he'll find himself in possession of a white elephant. Every dealer of reputation, in every part of the world, who is likely to deal in such things knows the Datchet diamonds as well as, if not better than, the Duke himself. The chap who has them will have to sell them to a fence. That fence will give him no more for them than if they were the commonest trumpery. And for this very good reason—the fence will either have to lock them up, and bequeath them to his great-grandson, on the offchance of his having face enough to put them on the market; or else he will have to break them up and offer them to the trade as if they were the ordinary stones of commerce, just turned up by the shovel. If I were on the cross, Mr. Paxton, I wouldn't have those sparklers if they were offered me for nothing. I should be able to get very little for them; the odds are they would quod me; and you may take this from me, that for the man—I don't care who he is, first offender or not—who is found with the Duchess of Datchet's diamonds in his possession, it's a lifer!"

Mr. Paxton was silent for a moment or two after the detective had ceased. He took another drink; it might have been that his lips stood in need of being moistened.

"You think it would be a lifer, do you?"

"I'm certain. After all the jewel thieves who have got clean off, if a judge does get this gentleman in front of him—which I think he will!—he'll make it as hot for him as ever he can. I shouldn't like to see you in such a position, Mr. Paxton, I assure you."

Again Mr. Paxton raised his glass to his lips.

"I hope that you won't, Mr. Ireland, with all my heart."

"I hope I sha'n't, Mr. Paxton. You know, perhaps as well as I do, it's an awful position for a man to stand in. What did you say your friend's name was—Lawrence? It's queer that I should have thought that I knew his face, and yet I don't think that I ever knew any one of that name. By the way, I fancy that you once told me that you didn't mind having a try at anything in which there was money to be made. Now, if you could give me a hint as to the whereabouts of the Duchess's diamonds, you might find that there was money in that."

As he emptied his glass Mr. Paxton looked the detective in the face.

"I wish I could, John—I'd be on for the deal! Only, I'm sorry that I can't."

CHAPTER VI

THE ADVENTURES OF A NIGHT

"There was something about Mr. John Ireland's manner which I couldn't quite make out."

This was what Mr. Paxton told himself as he came out of the Bodega. He turned down Ship Street, on to the front, meaning to stroll along the King's Road to his hotel. As he came out of the hotel his eye caught a glimpse of a loiterer standing in the shadow of a door higher up the street. When he had gone a little distance along the King's Road, glancing over his shoulder, he perceived that some one was standing at the corner of Ship Street, with his face turned in his direction.

"It occurs to me as being just possible that the events of the night are going to form a fitting climax to a day of adventure. That Ireland can have the slightest inkling of how the case really stands is certainly impossible; and yet, if I didn't know it was impossible, I should feel just a trifle uneasy. His manner's queer. I wonder if he has any suspicions of Lawrence, or of Lawrence's friend. That he knew the pair I'll bet my boots. Plainly, Lawrence is not the fellow's real name; it is simply the name by which he chose to be known to Daisy. If Ireland has cause to suspect the precious pair, seeing me with them twice, under what may seem to him to be curious circumstances, may cause him to ask himself what the deuce I am doing in such a galley. Undoubtedly, there was something in Mr. Ireland's manner which suggested that, in his opinion, I knew more about the matter than I altogether ought to."

Again Mr. Paxton glanced over his shoulder. About a hundred yards behind him a man advanced in his direction. Looking across the road, on the seaward side, he perceived that another man was there—a man who, as soon as Mr. Paxton turned his head, stopped short, seeming to be wholly absorbed in watching the sea. The man immediately behind him, however, was still advancing. Mr. Paxton hesitated. A fine rain was falling. It was late for Brighton. Except these two, not a creature was in sight.

"I wonder if either of those gentlemen is shadowing me, and, if so, which?"

He turned up West Street. When he had gone some way up it he peeped to see. A man was coming up the same side of the street on which he was.

"There's Number One." He went farther; then looked again. The same man was coming on; at the corner of the street a second man was loitering. "There's Number Two. Unless I am mistaken that is the gentleman who on a sudden found himself so interested in the sea. The question is, whether they are both engaged by the same person, or if they are in separate employ. I have no doubt whatever that one of them defies the chances of catching cold in the interests of Mr. Lawrence. Until the little mystery connected with the disappearance of his Gladstone bag is cleared up, if he can help it, he is scarcely likely to allow me to escape his constant supervision. For him I am prepared; but to be attended also by a myrmidon of Ireland's is, I confess, a prospect which I do not relish."

He trudged up the hill, pondering as he went. The rain was falling faster. He pulled his coat collar up about his ears. He had no umbrella.

"This is for me an experience of an altogether novel kind, and uncommonly pleasant weather it is in which to make its acquaintance. One obvious reason why Mr. Lawrence should have me shadowed is because of the strong desire which he doubtless feels to know where it is that I am staying. The natural deduction being that where I stay, there also stays my Gladstone bag. The odds are that Mr. Lawrence feels a quite conceivable curiosity to know in what the difference exactly consists between my Gladstone bag, and the one from which he, as he puts it, for a time has parted. Why John Ireland should wish to have my movements dogged I do not understand; and I am bound to add I would much rather not know either."

Mr. Paxton had reached the top of West Street. The man on the same side of the road still plodded along. On the opposite side of the street, much farther behind, came the other man too. Mr. Paxton formed an immediate resolution.

"I have no intention of tramping the streets of Brighton to see which of us can be tired first. I'm off indoors. The Gladstone, with its contents, I'll confide to the landlord of the hotel, to hold in his safe keeping. Then we'll see what will happen."

He swept round the corner into North Street, turning his face again towards the front. As he expected, first one follower, then the other, appeared.

"It's the second beggar who bothers me. I wonder what it means?"

Arrived at the hotel, Mr. Paxton went straight to the office. He asked for the landlord. He was told that the landlord did not reside in the building, but that he could see the manager. He saw the manager.

"I have property of considerable value in my Gladstone bag. Have you a strong room in which you could keep it for me till the morning?"

The manager replied in the affirmative, adding that he was always pleased to take charge of valuables which guests might commit to his charge. Mr. Paxton went to his bedroom. He unlocked the Gladstone bag—again with some difficulty—unwrapped the evening paper which served as an unworthy covering for such priceless treasures. There they were—a sight to gladden a connoisseur's heart; to make the blood in his veins run faster! How they sparkled, and glittered, and gleamed! How they threw off coruscations, each one a fresh revelation of beauty, with every movement of his hands and of his eyes. He would get nothing for them—was that what John Ireland said? Nothing, at any rate, but the lowest market price, as for the commonest gems. John Ireland's correctness remained to be proved. There were ways and means in which a man in his position—a man of reputation and of the world—could dispose of such merchandise, of which perhaps John Ireland, with all his knowledge of the shady side of life, had never dreamed.

Putting the stones back into the bag, Mr. Paxton took the bag down into the office. Then he went into the smoking-room. It was empty when he entered. But hardly had he settled himself in a chair, than some one else came in, a short, broad-shouldered individual, with piercing black eyes and shaven chin and cheeks. Mr. Paxton did not fancy his appearance; the man's manner, bearing, and attire were somewhat rough; he looked rather like a prizefighter than the sort of guest one would expect to encounter in an hotel of standing. Still less was Mr. Paxton pleased with the familiarity of his address. The man, placing himself in the adjoining chair, plunged into the heart of a conversation as if they had been the friends of years. After making one or two remarks, which were of so extremely confidential a nature that Mr. Paxton hardly knew whether to smile at them as the mere gaucheries of an ill-bred person, or to openly resent them as an intentional impertinence, the man began to subject him to a species of cross-examination which caused him to eye the presumptuous stranger with suddenly aroused but keen suspicion.

"Stopping here?"

"It seems that I am, doesn't it?"

"On what floor?"

"Why do you ask?"

"On the third floor, ain't you?"

"Why should you suppose that I am on the third floor?"

"I don't suppose nothing. Perhaps you're on the fourth. Are you on the fourth?"

"The world is full of possibilities."

The man took a pull or two at his pipe; then, wholly unabashed, began again—

"What's your number?"

"My number?"

"What's the number of your room?"

"I see."

"Well—what is it?"

"What is what?"

"What is what! Why, what's the number of your room?"

"Precisely."

"Well, you haven't told me what it is."

"No."

"Aren't you going to tell me?"

"I am afraid that I must wish you good-night." Rising, Mr. Paxton moved towards the door. Turning in his chair, the stranger stared at him with an air of grievance.

"You don't seem very polite, not answering a civil question when you're asked one."

Mr. Paxton only smiled.

"Good-night."

He could hear the stranger grumbling to himself, even after the door was closed. He asked the porter in the hall casually who the man might be.

"I don't know, sir. He came in just after you. I don't think I have ever seen him before. He has taken a bed for the night."

Mr. Paxton went up the stairs, smiling to himself as he went.

"They are hot on the scent. Mr. Lawrence evidently has no intention of allowing the grass to grow under his feet. He means, if the thing is possible, to have a sight of that Gladstone bag, at any rate by deputy. I may be wrong, but the deputy whom I fancy he has selected is an individual possessed of such a small amount of tact—whatever other virtues he may have—that I hardly think I am. In any case it is probably just as well that that Gladstone bag sleeps downstairs, while I sleep up."

The door of Mr. Paxton's bedroom was furnished with a bolt as well as a lock. He carefully secured both.

"I don't think that any one will be able to get through that door without arousing me. And even should any enterprising person succeed in doing so, I fear that his success will go no farther. His labours will be unrewarded."

Mr. Paxton was master of a great art—the art of being able to go to sleep when he wished. Practically, in bed or out of it, whenever he chose, he could treat himself to the luxury of a slumber; and also, when he chose, he could wake out of it. This very desirable accomplishment did not fail him then. As soon as he was between the sheets he composed himself to rest; and in an infinitesimally short space of time rest came to him. He slept as peacefully as if he had not had a care upon his mind.

And his sleep continued far into the night. But, profound and restful though it was, it was light. The slightest unusual sound was sufficient to awake him. It was indeed a sound which would have been inaudible to nine sleepers out of ten which actually did arouse him. Instantly his eyes were wide open and his senses keenly on the alert. He lay quite still in bed, listening. And as he listened he smiled.

"I thought so. My friend of the smoking-room, unless I err. Trying to turn the key in the lock with a pair of nippers, from outside. It won't do, my man. You are a little clumsy at your work. Your clumsiness betrayed you. You should get a firm hold of the key before you begin to turn, or your nippers are apt to slip, and when they slip they make a noise."

Mr. Paxton permitted no sign to escape him which could show the intruder who was endeavouring to make an unceremonious entrance into the apartment that he had ceased to sleep. He continued to lie quite still and to listen, enjoying what he heard. Either the lock was rusty or the key refractory, or, as Mr. Paxton said, the operator clumsy, but certainly he did take what seemed to be an unconscionable length of time in performing what is supposed to be a rudimentary function in the burglar's art. He fumbled and fumbled, time after time, in vain. One could hear in the prevailing silence the tiny click which his nippers made each time they lost their hold. Some three or four minutes probably elapsed before a slight grating sound—which seemed to show that the lock was rusty—told that, after all, the key had been turned. Mr. Paxton almost chuckled.

"Now for the scattering of the labourer's hopes of harvest!"

The person who was outside the door, satisfied that the lock had been opened, firmly, yet no doubt gently, grasped the handle of the door. He turned it. With all his gentleness it grated. One could hear that he gave it an inward push, only to discover that the bolt was shot inside. And that same moment Mr. Paxton's voice rang out, clear and cold—

"Who's there?"

No answer. Mr. Paxton's sharp ears imagined that they could just detect the shuffling along the passage of retreating footsteps.

"Is any one at the door?"

Still no reply. Mr. Paxton's next words were uttered sotto voce with a grin.

"I don't fancy that there is any one outside the door just now; nor that to-night there is likely to be again. I'll just jump out and undo the result of that poor man's patient labours."

Re-locking the door, Mr. Paxton once more composed himself to rest, and again sleep came to him almost in the instant that he sought it. And for the second time he was aroused by a sound so faint that it would hardly have penetrated to the average sleeper's senses. On this occasion the interruption was unexpected. He turned himself slightly in bed, so that he might be in a better position for listening.

"What's that? If it's my friend of the smoking-room again, he's a persevering man. It doesn't sound as if it were coming from the door; it sounds more as if it were coming from the window—and, by George, it is! What does it mean? It occurs to me that this is a case in which it might be advisable that I should make personal inquiries."

Slipping out of bed, Mr. Paxton thrust his legs into a pair of trousers. He took a revolver from underneath his pillow.

"It's lucky," he said to himself, as his fingers closed upon the weapon, "that my prophetic soul told me that this was a plaything which might be likely to come in handy."

In his bare feet he moved towards the window, holding the revolver in his hand.

The room was in darkness, but Mr. Paxton was aware that in front of the window stood the dressing-table. He knew also that the window itself was screened, not only by the blind, but by a pair of heavy curtains. Placing himself by the side of the dressing-table, he gingerly moved one of the curtains, with a view of ascertaining if his doing so would enable him to see what was going on without. One thing the movement of the curtains did reveal to him, that there was a dense fog out of doors. The blind did not quite fit the window, and enough space was left at the side to show that the lights in the King's Road were veiled by a thick white mist. Mr. Paxton moved both the blind and the curtain sufficiently aside to enable him to see all that there was to be seen, without, however, unnecessarily exposing himself.

For a moment or so that all was nothing. Then, gradually becoming accustomed to the light, or want of it, he saw something which, while little enough in itself, was yet sufficient to have given a nervous person a considerable shock. Something outside seemed to reach from top to bottom of the window. At first Mr. Paxton could not make out what it was. Then he understood.

"A ladder—by George, it is! It would almost seem as if my friend of the smoking-room had given his friends outside the 'office,' and that they are taking advantage of the fog to endeavor to succeed where he has failed. If I had expected this kind of thing, I should have preferred to sleep a little nearer to the sky. Instead of the first floor, it should have been the third, or even the fourth, beyond the reach of ladders. Messrs. Lawrence and Co. seem resolved to beat the iron while it's hot. The hunt becomes distinctly keen. It is perhaps only natural to expect that they should be anxious; but, so far as I am concerned, a little of this sort of thing suffices. They are slow at getting to work, considering how awkward they might find it if some one were to come along and twig that ladder. Hallo, the fun begins! Unless my ears deceive me, some one's coming now."

Mr. Paxton's ears did not deceive him. Even as he spoke a dark something appeared on the ladder above the level of the window. It was a man's head. The head was quickly followed by a body. The acute vision of the unseen watcher could dimly make out, against the white background of fog, the faint outline of a man's figure. This figure did an unexpected thing. Without any sort of warning, the shutter of a dark lantern was suddenly opened, and the light thrown on the window in such a way that it shone full into Mr. Paxton's eyes. That gentleman retained his presence of mind. He withdrew his head, while keeping his hold on the blind; if he had let it go the movement could scarcely have failed to have been perceived.

The light vanished almost as quickly as it came. It was followed by a darkness which seemed even denser than before. It was a second or two before Mr. Paxton could adapt his dazzled eyes to the restoration of the blackness. When he did so, he perceived that the man on the ladder was leaning over towards the window. If the lantern had been flashed on him just then, it would have been seen that an ugly look was on Mr. Paxton's countenance.

"You startled me, you brute, with your infernal lantern, and now I've half a mind to startle you."

Mr. Paxton made his half-mind a whole one. He brought his revolver to the level of his elbow; he pointed it at the window, and he fired. The figure on the ladder disappeared with the rapidity of a jack-in-the-box. Whether the man had fallen or not, there was for the moment no evidence to show. Mr. Paxton dragged the dressing-table away, threw up the window, and looked out. The mist came streaming in. In the distance could be heard the stampede of feet. Plainly two or three persons were making off as fast as their heels would carry them. An imperious knocking came at the bedroom door.

"Anything the matter in there?"

Mr. Paxton threw the door wide open. A porter was standing in the lighted corridor.

"A good deal's the matter. Burglary's the matter."

"Burglary?"

"Yes, burglary. I caught a man in the very act of opening my window, so I had a pop at him. He appears to have got off; but his ladder he has left behind."

Other people came into the room, among them the manager. An examination of the premises was made from without. The man had escaped; but the precipitancy of his descent was evidenced by the fact that his lantern, falling from his grasp, had been shattered to fragments on the ground.

The fragments he had not stayed to gather. Still less had he and his associates stood on the order of their going sufficiently long to enable them to remove the ladder.

CHAPTER VII

THE DATCHET DIAMONDS ARE PLACED IN SAFE CUSTODY

When the morning came, and Mr. Paxton found himself being cross-examined by the manager, with every probability of his, later on, having to undergo an examination by the police, he was as taciturn as possible. Although he was by no means sorry that he had fired that shot, and so effectually frightened the man upon the ladder, he would infinitely rather that less fuss had been made about it afterwards.

One thing Mr. Paxton had decided to do before he left his bedroom. He had decided to remove the Datchet diamonds to a place of safety. That Mr. Lawrence and his friends had a very shrewd notion that they were in his possession was plain; that they were disposed to stick at nothing which would enable them to get hold of them again was, if possible, plainer. Mr. Paxton was resolute that they should not have them, who ever did.

It happened that, in his more prosperous days, he had rented one of the Chancery Lane Deposit Company's safes. Nor was the term of his tenancy at an end. He determined to do a bold, and, one might add, an impudent thing. He would carry the duchess' diamonds back with him to town, lock them in the safe he rented, and then, whatever might happen, nobody but himself would ever be able to have access to them again. He had the Gladstone bag brought up to his bedroom, removed from it the precious parcel, returned the bag itself to the manager's keeping, and, declining to have his morning meal at the hotel, went up by the Pullman train to town, and breakfasted on board. He flattered himself that whoever succeeded in taking from him the diamonds before his arrival with them in Chancery Lane, would have to be a very clever person.

Still, he did not manage to reach his journey's end without having had one or two little adventures by the way.

He drove up from the hotel to the station in a hansom cab. As he stepped into the cab he noticed, standing on the kerbstone a little to the left of the hotel entrance, a man who wore his billycock a good deal on the side of his head, and who had a cigar sticking out of the corner of his mouth.

He should not have particularly observed the fellow had not the man, as soon as he found Mr. Paxton's eyes turned in his direction, performed a right-about-face on his heels, and presented an almost ostentatious view of the middle of the back. When Mr. Paxton's cab rattled into the central yard, and Mr. Paxton proceeded to step out from it on to the pavement, another hansom came dashing up behind his own, and from it there alighted the man who had turned his back on him in front of the hotel. As Mr. Paxton took his ticket this man was at his side. And, having purchased his morning paper, as he strolled up the platform towards the train, he noticed that the fellow was only a few steps in his rear.

There seemed to be no reasonable room for doubt that the man was acting as his shadow. No one likes to feel that he is under espionage. And Mr. Paxton in particular felt that just recently he had endured enough of that kind of thing to last—if his own tastes were to be consulted—for the remainder of his life. He decided to put a stop there and then to, at any rate, this man's persecution. Suddenly standing still, wheeling sharply round, Mr. Paxton found himself face to face with the individual with his hat on the side of his head.

"Are you following me?"

Mr. Paxton's manner as he asked the question, though polite, meant mischief. The other seemed to be a little taken aback. Then, with an impudent air, taking what was left of his cigar out of his mouth, he blew a volume of smoke full into Mr. Paxton's eyes.

"Were you speaking to me?"

Mr. Paxton's fingers itched to knock the smoker down. But situated as he was, a row in public just then would have been sheer madness. He adopted what was probably an even more effective plan. He signalled to a passing official.

"Guard!" The man approached. "This person has been following me from my hotel. Be so good as to call a constable. His proceedings require explanation."

The man began to bluster.

"What do you mean by saying I've been following you? Who are you, I should like to know? Can't any one move about except yourself? Following you, indeed! It's more likely that you've been following me!"

A constable came up. Mr. Paxton addressed him in his cool, incisive tones.

"Officer, this person has followed me from my hotel to the station; from the station to the booking-office; from the booking-office to the bookstall; and now he is following me from the bookstall to the train. I have some valuable property on me, with which fact he is possibly acquainted. Since he is a complete stranger to me, I should be obliged if you would ask him what is the cause of the unusual interest which he appears to take in my movements."

The man with the cigar became apologetic.

"The gentleman's quite mistaken; I'm not following him; I wouldn't do such a thing! I'm going to town by this train, and it seems that this gentleman's going too, and perhaps that's what's made him think that I was following. If there's any offence, I'm sure that I beg pardon."

The man held out his hand—it was unclean and it was big—as if expecting Mr. Paxton to grasp it. Mr. Paxton, however, moved away addressing a final observation to the constable as he went.

"Officer, be so good as to keep an eye upon that man."

Mr. Paxton entered the breakfast carriage. What became of the too attentive stranger he neither stopped to see nor cared to inquire. He saw no more of him; that was all he wanted. As the train rushed towards town he ate his breakfast and he read his paper.

The chief topic of interest in the journals of the day was the robbery on the previous afternoon of the Duchess of Datchet's diamonds. It filled them to the almost complete exclusion of other news of topical importance. There were illustrations of some of the principal jewels which had been stolen, together with anecdotes touching on their history—very curious some of them were! The Dukes of Datchet seemed to have gathered those beautiful gems, if not in ways which were dark, then occasionally, at any rate, in ways which were, to say the least of it, peculiar. Those glittering pebbles seemed to have been mixed up with a good deal of trickery and fraud and crime.

The papers gave the most minute description of the more important stones. Even the merest novice in the knowledge of brilliants, if he had mastered those details, could scarcely fail to recognise them if ever they came his way. It appeared that few even royal collections possessed so large a number of really fine examples. Their valuation at a quarter of a million was the purest guesswork. The present duke would not have accepted for them twice that sum.

Half a million! Five hundred thousand pounds! At even 3 per cent.—and who does not want more for his money than a miserable 3 per cent.?— that was fifteen thousand pounds a year. Three hundred pounds a week. More than forty pounds a day. Over three pounds for every working hour. And Mr. Paxton had it in his pockets!

It was not strange that Mr. Lawrence and his associates should betray such lively anxiety to regain possession of such a sum as that; it would have been strange if they had not! It was a sum worth having; worth fighting for; worth risking something for as well.

And yet there was something; indeed, there was a good deal, which could be said for the other side of the question. Mr. Paxton owned to himself that there was. He could not honestly—if it were still possible to speak of honesty in connection with a gentleman who had launched himself on such a venture—lay his hand upon his heart, and say that he was happier since he had discovered what were the contents of somebody else's Gladstone bag. On the contrary, if he could have blotted out of his life the few hours which had intervened since the afternoon of the previous day, he would have done so, even yet, with a willing hand.

Nor was this feeling lessened by an incident which took place on his arrival at London Bridge. If he were of an adventurous turn of mind, evidently he could not have adopted a more certain means of gratifying his peculiar taste than by retaining possession of the duchess's diamonds. Adventures were being heaped on him galore.

As he was walking down the platform, looking for a likely cab, some one came rushing up against him from behind with such violence as to send him flying forward on his face. Two roughly dressed men assisted him to rise. But, while undergoing their kindly ministrations, it occurred to him, in spite of his half-dazed condition, that they were evincing a livelier interest in the contents of his pockets than in his regaining his perpendicular. He managed to shake them off, however, before their interest had been carried to too generous a length.

The inevitable crowd had gathered. A man, attired as a countryman, was volubly explaining—with a volubility which was hardly suggestive of a yokel—that he was late for market, and was hurrying along without looking where he was going, when he stumbled against the gentleman, and was so unfortunate as to knock him over. He was profuse, and indeed almost lachrymose, in his apologies for the accident which his clumsiness had occasioned. Mr. Paxton said nothing. He did not see what there was to say. He dusted himself down, adjusted his hat, got into a cab and drove away.

Drove straight away to Chancery Lane. And, when he had deposited the Duchess of Datchet's diamonds in his safe, and had left them behind him in that impregnable fortress, where, if the statements of the directors could be believed, fire could not penetrate, nor water, nor rust, nor thieves break through and steal, he felt as if a load had been lifted off his mind.

CHAPTER VIII

IN THE MOMENT OF HIS SUCCESS

Diamonds worth a quarter of a million! And yet already they were beginning to hang like a millstone round Mr. Paxton's neck. The relief which he felt at having got rid of them from his actual person proved to be but temporary. All day they haunted him. Having done the one thing which he had come to town to do, he found himself unoccupied. He avoided the neighbourhood of the Stock Exchange, and of his usual haunts, for reasons. Eries were still declining. The difference against him had assumed a portentous magnitude. Possibly, confiding brokers were seeking for him high and low, anxious for security which would protect them against the necessity of having to make good his losses. No, just then the City was not for him. Discretion, of a sort, suggested his confining himself to the West-end of town.

Unfortunately, in this case, the West-end meant loitering about bars and similar stimulating places. He drank not only to kill time but also to drown his thoughts, and the more he tried to drown them, the more they floated on the surface.

What a fool he had been—what an egregious fool! How he had exchanged his talents for nothing, and for less than nothing. How he had thrown away his prospects, his opportunities, his whole life, his all! And now, by way of a climax, he had been guilty of a greater folly than any which had gone before. He had sold more than his birthright for less—much less—than a mess of pottage. He had lost his soul for the privilege of being able to hang a millstone round his neck—cast honour to the winds for the sake of encumbering himself with a burden which would crush him lower and lower, until it laid him level with the dust.

Wherever he went, the story of the robbery met his eyes. The latest news of it was announced on the placards of the evening papers. Newsboys bawled it in his ears. He had only to listen to what was being said by the other frequenters of the bars against which he lounged to learn that it was the topic of conversation on every tongue. All England, all Europe, indeed, one might say that the whole of the civilised world was on tiptoe to catch the man who had done this thing. As John Ireland had said, he might as soon think of being able to sell the diamonds as of being able to sell the Koh-i-Nor. Every one who knew anything at all of precious stones was on the look-out for them, from pole to pole. During his lifetime he would not even venture to attempt their disposal, any attempt of the kind would inevitably involve his being instantaneously branded as a felon.

Last night, when he left London, he had had something over two hundred pounds in his pockets. Except debts, and certain worthless securities, for which no one would give him a shilling, it was all he had left in the world. It was not a large sum, but it was sufficient to take him to the other side of the globe, and to keep him there until he had had time to turn himself round, and to find some means of earning for himself his daily bread. He had proposed to go on to Southampton this morning, thence straight across the seas. Now what was it he proposed to do? Every day that he remained in England meant making further inroads into his slender capital. At the rate at which he was living, it would rapidly dwindle all away. Then how did he intend to replenish it? By selling the duchess's diamonds? Nonsense! He told himself, with bitter frankness, that such an idea was absolute nonsense; that such a prospect was as shadowy as, and much more dangerous than, the proverbial mirage of the desert.

He returned by an afternoon train to Brighton, in about as black a mood as he could be. He sat in a corner of a crowded compartment—for some reason he rather shirked travelling alone—communing with the demons of despair who seemed to be the tenants of his brain; fighting with his own particular wild beasts. Arrived at Brighton without adventure, he drove straight to Makell's Hotel.

As he advanced into the hall, the manager came towards him out of the office.

"Good evening, Mr. Paxton. Did you authorise any one to come and fetch away your bag?"

"No. Why?"

"Some fellow came and said that you had sent him for your Gladstone bag."

"I did nothing of the kind. Did you give it him?"

The manager smiled.

"Hardly. You had confided it to my safe keeping, and I was scarcely likely to hand it to a stranger who was unable to present a more sufficient authority than he appeared to have. We make it a rule that articles entrusted to our charge are returned to the owners only, on personal application."

"What sort of a man was he to look at?"

"Oh, a shabby-looking chap, very much down at heel indeed, middle-aged; the sort of man whom you would expect would run messages."

"Tell me, as exactly as you can, what it was he said."

"He said that Mr. Paxton had sent him for his Gladstone bag. I asked him where you were. He said you were at Medina Villas, and you wanted your bag. You had given him a shilling to come for it, and you were to give him another shilling when he took it back. I told him our rule referring to property deposited with us by guests, and he made off."

Medina Villas? Miss Strong resided in Medina Villas, and Miss Wentworth; with which fact Mr. Lawrence was possibly acquainted. Once more in this latest dash for the bag Mr. Paxton seemed to trace that gentleman's fine Roman hand. He thanked the manager for the care which he had taken of his interests.

"I'm glad that you sent the scamp empty away, but, between you and me, the loss wouldn't have been a very serious one if you had given him what he wanted. I took all that the bag contained of value up with me to town, and left it there."

The manager looked at him, as Mr. Paxton felt, a trifle scrutinisingly, as if he could not altogether make him out.

"There seems to be a sort of dead set made at you. First, the attempted burglary last night—which is a kind of thing which has never before been known in the whole history of the hotel—and now this impudent rascal trying to make out that you had authorised him to receive your Gladstone bag. One might almost think that you were carrying something about with you which was of unique importance, and that the fact of your doing so had somehow become known to a considerable proportion of our criminal population."

Mr. Paxton laughed. He had the bag carried upstairs, telling himself as he went that it was already more than time that his sojourn at Makell's Hotel should be brought to a conclusion.

He ate a solitary dinner, lingering over it, though he had but a scanty appetite, as long as he could, in order to while away the time until the hour came for meeting Daisy. Towards the end of the meal, sick to death of his own thoughts, for sheer want of something else to do, he took up an evening paper, which he had brought into the room with him, and which was lying on a chair at his side, and began to glance at it. As he idly skimmed its columns, all at once a paragraph in the City article caught his eye. He read the words with a feeling of surprise; then, with increasing amazement, he read them again.

"The boom in the shares of the Trumpit Gold Mine continues. On the strength of a report that the reef which has been struck is of importance, the demand for them, even at present prices, exceeded the supply. When our report left, buyers were offering £10—the highest price of the day."

After subjecting the paragraph to a second reading, Mr. Paxton put the paper down upon his knees, and gasped for breath. It was a mistake—a canard—quite incredible. Trumpits selling at £10—it could not be! He would have been glad, quite lately, to have sold his for 10d each; only he was conscious that even at that price he would have found no buyer. £10 indeed! It was a price of which, at one time, he had dreamed—but it had remained a dream.

He read the paragraph again. So far as the paper was concerned, there seemed to be no doubt about it—there it was in black and white. The paper was one of the highest standing, of unquestionable authority, not given to practical jokes—especially in the direction of quotations in its City article. Could the thing be true? He felt that something was tingling all over his body. On a sudden, his pulses had begun to beat like sledge-hammers. He rose from his seat, just as the waiter was placing still another plate in front of him, and, to the obvious surprise of that well-trained functionary, he marched away without a word. He made for the smoking-room. He knew that he should find the papers there. And he found them, morning and evening papers—even some of the papers of the day before—as many as he wished. He ransacked them all. Each, with one accord, told the same tale.

The thing might be incredible, but it was true!

While he was gambling in Eries, losing all, and more than all, that he had; while he was gambling in stolen jewels, losing all that was left of his honour too, a movement had been taking place in the market which was making his fortune for him all the time, and he had not noticed it. The thing seemed to him to be almost miraculous. And certainly it was not the least of the miracles which lately had come his way.

Some two years before a friend had put him on—as friends do put us on—to a real good thing—the Trumpit Gold Mine. The friend professed to have special private information about this mine, and Mr. Paxton believed that he had. He still believed that he thought he had. Mr. Paxton was not a greenhorn, but he was a gambler, which now and then is about as bad. He looked at the thing all round—in the light of his friend's special information!—as far as he could, and as time would permit, and it seemed to him to be good enough for a plunge. The shares just then were at a discount—a considerable discount. From one point of view it was the time to buy them—and he did. He got together pretty well every pound he could lay his hands on, and bought ten thousand—bought them out and out, to hold—and went straight off and told Miss Strong he had made his fortune. It was only the mistake of a word—what he ought to have told her was that he had lost it. The certainly expected find of yellow ore did not come off, nor did the looked-for rise in the shares come off either. They continued at a discount, and went still lower. Purchasers could not be discovered at any price.

It was a bitter blow. Almost, if not quite, as bitter a blow to Miss Strong as to himself. Indeed, Mr. Paxton had felt ever since as if Miss Strong had never entirely forgiven him for having made such a fool of her. He might—he could not help fancying that some such line of reasoning had occupied her attention more than once—before telling her of the beautiful chickens which were shortly about to be hatched, at least have waited till the eggs were laid.

He had been too much engaged in other matters to pay attention to quotations for shares, which had long gone unquoted, and which he had, these many days, regarded as a loss past praying for. It appeared that rumours had come of gold in paying quantities having been found; that the rumours had gathered strength; that, in consequence, the shares had risen, until, on a sudden, the market was in a frenzy—as occasionally the market is apt to be—and ten pounds a-piece was being offered. Ten thousand at ten pounds a-piece—why, it was a hundred thousand pounds! A fortune in itself!

By the time Mr. Paxton had attained to something like an adequate idea of the situation, he was half beside himself with excitement. He looked at his watch—it was time for meeting Daisy. He hurried into the hall, crammed on his hat, and strode into the street.

Scarcely had he taken a dozen steps, when some one struck him a violent blow from behind. As he turned to face his assailant, an arm was thrust round his neck, and what felt like a damp cloth was forced against his mouth. He was borne off his feet, and, in spite of his struggles, was conveyed with surprising quickness into a cab which was drawn up against the kerb.

CHAPTER IX

A PROPOSAL OF MARRIAGE

"It's too bad of him!"

Miss Strong felt that it was much too bad! Twenty minutes after the appointed time, and still no signs of Mr. Paxton. The weather was, if anything, worse even than the night before. The mist was more pronounced; a chillier breeze was in the air; a disagreeable drizzle showed momentary symptoms of falling faster. The pier was nearly deserted; it was not the kind of evening to tempt pleasure-seekers out.

Miss Strong had been at the place of meeting in front of time. After Mr. Paxton's departure on the previous evening, between Miss Wentworth and herself there had been certain passages. Bitter words had been said—particularly by Miss Strong. In consequence, for the first time on record, the friends had parted in anger. Nor had the quarrel been made up afterwards. On the contrary, all day long the atmosphere had been charged with electricity. Miss Strong was conscious that in certain of the things which she had said she had wronged her friend, as, she assured herself, her friend had wronged her lover. It is true two wrongs do not make a right; but Miss Strong had made up her mind that she would not apologise to Miss Wentworth for what she had said to her, until Miss Wentworth had apologised for what she had said to Cyril. As Miss Wentworth showed no disposition to do anything of the kind, the position was more than a trifle strained. So strained indeed that Miss Strong, after confining herself to the bedroom for most of the day, rushed out of the house a full hour before it was time for meeting Cyril, declaring to herself that anything—mist, wind, or rain—was better than remaining prisoned any longer under the same roof which sheltered an unfriendly friend. Under such circumstances, to her, it seemed a cardinal crime on Cyril's part that he should actually be twenty minutes late.

"After what he said last night, about not keeping me waiting for a second—considering the way in which he said it—I did think that he would be punctual. How can he expect me to trust him in larger things, if he does not keep faith with me in small? If anything had happened to detain him, he might have let me know in time."

The indignant lady did not stay to reflect that she had left home unnecessarily early, and that an explanation of the gentleman's absence might, even now, be awaiting her there. Besides, twenty minutes is not long. But perhaps in the case of a lovers' rendezvous, by some magnifying process proper to such occasions, twenty minutes may assume the dimensions of an hour.

"I'll go once more up and down the pier, and then if he hasn't come I'll go straight home. How Charlie will laugh at me, and triumph, and say 'I told you so!' Oh, Cyril, how unkind you are, not to come when you promised! I don't care, but I do know this, that if Charlie Wentworth is not careful what she says, I will never speak to her again—never—as long as I live!"

It seemed as if the young lady did not quite know whether to be the more angry with her lover or her friend. She went up the pier; then started to return. As she came back a man wearing a mackintosh advanced to her with uplifted cap and outstretched hand.

"Miss Strong!"

It was Mr. Lawrence. The last man whom, just then, she would have wished to see.

Could anything have been more unfortunate? What would Cyril think if, again, he found them there together. She decided to get rid of the man without delay. But the thing was easier decided on than done. Especially as Mr. Lawrence immediately said something which caused her to postpone his dismissal longer than she had intended.

"I saw Mr. Paxton this afternoon, in town."

He had fallen in quite naturally by her side. She had moderated her pace, wishing to rid herself of him before she reached the gates.

"Indeed! In the City, I suppose? He is there on business."

"He wasn't in the City when I saw him. And the business on which he was employed was of an agreeable kind. He seemed to be making a day of it at the Criterion bar."

"Are you not mistaken? Are you sure that it was Mr. Paxton?"

"Quite sure. May I ask if he is an intimate friend of yours?"

"He is—a very intimate friend indeed. I am expecting him here every moment."

"Expecting him here! You really are!" Mr. Lawrence stopped, and turned, and stared, as if her words surprised him. "I beg your pardon, Miss Strong, but—he is stopping to-night in town."

"Stopping to-night in town!" It was Miss Strong's turn to stand and stare. "How do you know? Did he tell you so?"

"Not in so many words, but—I think you will find that he is. The—the fact is, Miss Strong, I heard an ugly story about Mr. Paxton, and—I am afraid you will find that there is something wrong."

The lady grasped the handle of her umbrella with added vigour. Her impulse was to lay it about the speaker's head. But she refrained.

"You must be too acute of hearing, Mr. Lawrence. If I were you, I should exchange your ears for another pair. Good evening."

But she was not to escape from him so easily. He caught her by the arm.

"Miss Strong, don't go—not for a moment. There is something which I particularly wish to say to you."

"What there is, Mr. Lawrence, which you can particularly wish to say to me I am unable to conceive."

"I fear that may be so, Miss Strong. But there is something, all the same. These are early days in which to say it; and the moment is not the most propitious I could have chosen. But circumstances are stronger than I. I have a feeling that it must be now or never. You know very little of me, Miss Strong. Probably you will say you know nothing—that I am, to all intents and purposes, a stranger. But I know enough of you to know that I love you: that you are to me what no woman has ever been before, or will ever be again. And what I particularly wish to say to you is to ask you to be my wife."

His words were so wholly unexpected, that, for the moment, they took the lady's breath away. He spoke quietly, even coldly; but, in his coldness there was a vibrant something which was suggestive of the heat of passion being hidden below, while the very quietude of his utterance made his words more effective than if he had shouted them at the top of his voice. It was a second or two before the startled lady answered.

"What you have said takes me so completely by surprise that I hardly know whether or not you are in earnest."

"I am in earnest, I assure you. That I am mad in saying it, I am quite aware; how mad, even you can have no notion. But I had to say it, and it's said. If you would only be my wife, you would do a good deed, of the magnitude of which you have no conception. There is nothing in return which I would not do for you. On this occasion in saying so I do not think that I am using an empty form of words."

"As you yourself pointed out, you are a stranger to me; nor have I any desire that you should be anything but a stranger."

"Thank you, Miss Strong."

"You brought it upon yourself."

"I own that it is not your fault that I love you; nor can I admit that it is my misfortune."

"There is one chief reason why your flattering proposals are unwelcome to me. I happen already to be a promised wife. I am engaged to Mr. Paxton."

"Is that so? Then I am sorry for you."

"Why are you sorry?"

"Ere long, unless I am mistaken, you will learn that I have cause for sorrow, and that you have cause for sorrow too."

Without another word the lady, the gentleman making no effort to detain her, walked away. She went straight home.

She found Miss Wentworth in her favourite attitude—feet stretched on a chair in front of her—engaged, as Miss Strong chose to phrase it, in "her everlasting reading." When Miss Wentworth was not writing she was wont to be reading. Miss Strong occasionally wished that she would employ herself in more varying occupations.

Momentarily oblivious of the coolness which had sprung up between her friend and herself, Miss Strong plumped herself down on to a chair, forgetful also of the fact that she had brought her umbrella with her into the room, and that the rain was trickling down it.

"Charlie, whatever do you think has happened?"

Miss Wentworth had contented herself with nodding as her friend had entered. Now, lowering her book, she glanced at her over the top of it.

"I don't know what has happened, my dear, but I do know what is happening—your umbrella is making a fish-pond on the carpet."

Miss Strong got up with something of a jump. She deposited her mackintosh and umbrella in the hall. When she returned her friend greeted her with laughter in her eyes.

"Well, what has happened? But perhaps before you tell me you might give an eye to those elegant boots of yours. They never struck me as being altogether waterproof."

With tightened lips Miss Strong removed her boots. It was true that they badly wanted changing. But that was nothing. In her present mood she resented having her attention diverted to unimportant details. She expressed herself to that effect as she undid the buttons.

"I do believe that you are the hardest-natured girl I ever knew. You've no sense of feeling. If I were dying for want of it, I should never dream of coming to you for sympathy."

Miss Wentworth received this tirade with complete placidity.

"Quite so, my dear. Well, what has happened?"

Miss Strong snuggled her feet into her slippers. She began to fidget about the room. Suddenly she burst out in what could only be described as a tone of angry petulance.

"You will laugh at me—I know you will. But you had better not. I can tell you that I am in no mood to be laughed at. I feel as if I must tell it to some one, and I have no one in the world to tell things to but you—Mr. Lawrence has dared to make me a proposal of marriage."

The complete, and one might almost say, the humorous repose of Miss Wentworth's manner was in striking contrast to her friend's excitability.

"Mr. Lawrence? Isn't that the individual whom you met on the Dyke, and who was introduced to you by his umbrella?"

"Of course it is!"

"And he has proposed to you, has he? Very good of him, I'm sure. The sex has scored another victory. I did not know that matters had progressed with you so far as that! But now and then, I suppose, one does move quickly. I offer you my congratulations."

"Charlie! You are maddening!"

"Not at all. But I believe that it is a popular theory that a woman ought always to be congratulated on receiving a proposal from a man. The idea seems to be that it is the best gift which the gods can possibly bestow—upon a woman. And, pray, where did this gentleman so honour you? Right under Mr. Paxton's nose?"

"Cyril wasn't there."

"Not there?" Miss Strong turned her face away. Miss Wentworth eyed her for a moment before she spoke again. "I thought that you had an appointment with him, and that you went out to keep it."

"He never came."

"Indeed!"

Miss Wentworth's tone was dry. But, in spite of its dryness, it seemed that there was something in it which touched a secret spring which was hidden in her listener's breast. Suddenly Miss Strong broke into a flood of tears, and, running forward, fell on her knees at her friend's side, and pillowed her face in her lap.

"Oh, Charlie, I am so unhappy—you mustn't laugh at me—I am! Everything seems to be going wrong—everything. I feel as if I should like to die!"

"There is allotted to every one of us a time for death. I wouldn't attempt to forestall my allotment, if I were you. What is the particular, pressing grief?"

"I am the most miserable girl in the world!"

"Hush! Be easy! There are girls—myriads of them—myriads—who would esteem such misery as yours happiness. Tell me, what's the trouble?"

In spite of the satirical touch which tinged her speech, a strain of curious melody had all at once come into her voice which—as if it had been an anæsthetic—served to ease the extreme tension of the other's nerves. Miss Strong looked up, the tears still streaming down her cheeks, but exhibiting some signs of at least elementary self-control.

"Everything's the trouble! Everything seems to be going wrong; that's just the plain and simple truth. Cyril said he would meet me tonight, and promised he'd be punctual, and I waited for him, ever so long, on the pier, in the rain, and after all he never came. And then that wretched Mr. Lawrence came and made his ridiculous proposal, and—and said all sorts of dreadful things of Cyril!"

"Said all sorts of dreadful things of Cyril, did he? As, for instance, what?"

"He said that he was going to stop in town all night."

"Well, and why shouldn't he?"

"Why shouldn't he? After saying he would meet me! And promising to be punctual! And keeping me waiting on the pier! Without giving me any sort of hint that he had changed his mind! Charlie!"

"Pray, how did Mr. Lawrence come to know that Mr. Paxton intended to spend the night in London?"

"He says that he saw him there."

"I did not know they were acquainted!"

"I introduced them the night before last."

"I see." Again Miss Wentworth's tone was significantly dry. "Mr. Paxton has never seemed to me to be a man whose confidence was easily gained, especially by a stranger. Mr. Lawrence must have progressed more rapidly with him even than with you. And, pray, what else was Mr. Lawrence pleased to say of Mr. Paxton?"

"Oh, a lot of lies! Of course I knew that they were a lot of lies, but they made me so wild that I felt that I should like to shake him."

"Shake me instead, my dear. One is given to understand that jolting is good for the liver. Who's that?"

There was a sound of knocking at the front door. Miss Strong glanced eagerly round. A flush came into her cheeks; a light into her eyes.

"Possibly that is the recalcitrant Mr. Paxton, in his own proper person, coming with apologies in both his hands. Perhaps you would like to go and see."

CHAPTER X

CYRIL'S FRIEND

Miss Strong did like to go and see. She looked at Miss Wentworth with a make-believe of anger, and, rising to her feet, went quickly across the room. Admission had already been given to the knocker. There advanced towards the girl standing in the open door a man—who was not Mr. Paxton.

"Mr. Franklyn! I thought—"

There was a note of disappointment in her voice. She stopped short, as if desirous not to allow her self-betrayal to go too far. She moved a little back, so as to allow the newcomer to enter the room.

This newcomer was a man of the medium height, about forty years of age. His black hair was already streaked with grey. He had a firm, clear-cut, clean-shaven mouth and chin, and a pair of penetrating grey-black eyes, with which he had a trick of looking every one whom he addressed squarely in the face. His manner, ordinarily, was grave and deliberate, as if he liked to weigh each word he uttered. He held Miss Strong's hand for a moment in his cool, close grasp.

"Well; you thought what?"

"I'm very glad to see you—you know I am; but I thought it was Cyril."

"Are you expecting him?"

"I was expecting him, but—it seems he hasn't come."

Turning to Miss Wentworth he greeted her. And it was to be noted that as she offered him her hand a humorous twinkle beamed through her glasses, and her whole face was lighted by a smile. He turned again to Miss Strong.

"Have you heard the news?"

"What news?"

"Hasn't Cyril told you?"

"He told me something last night, but I really couldn't tell you quite what it was he told me, and I haven't seen him since."

"He is in Brighton?"

"Is he? I was informed that he was stopping in town."

"You were informed? By whom?"

"By an acquaintance, who said that he saw him there."

Mr. Franklyn waited before speaking again. His unflinching eyes seemed to be studying the lady's face. Probably he saw that there was something unusual in her manner.

"That is strange. I was under the impression that he was in Brighton. I have come from town specially to see him. I expected to find him with you here."

"He did promise to meet me to-night. He hasn't kept his promise. I don't understand why. To be plain with you, it rather troubles me.

"He promised to meet you?"

"He did most faithfully."

"And you have received no intimation from him to the effect that he was not coming?"

"Not a word—not a line!"

"Then he may be here at any moment. Something has unexpectedly delayed him. You are acquainted with him sufficiently well to be aware that had anything occurred to cause him to alter his plans, he would immediately have let you know. Your informant was wrong. I have had inquiries made for him everywhere in town, and as a result have good reason to believe that he is in Brighton."

"What is the news of which you were speaking?"

"Has Cyril said nothing to you about the Trumpit Gold Mine?"

"He referred to it casually the night before last in his usual strain, as having been the cause of his destruction."

"That really is extraordinary. I confess I do not understand it. It is so unlike Cyril to have communicated neither with you nor with me. Are you sure that he said nothing more?"

"About the Trumpit Gold Mine? Not a word. What was there, what is there to say? Do get it out!"

The young lady made an impatient movement with her foot. The gentleman looked at her with amusement in his eyes. She was very well worth looking at just then. Her hair was a little out of order; and, though she might not have agreed with such a statement, it suited her when it was slightly disarranged. Her cheeks were flushed. She held herself very straight. Perhaps it was her tears which had lent brightness to her eyes; they were bright. Her small, white teeth sparkled between her blush-rose lips, which were slightly parted as if in repressed excitement. She presented a pretty picture of a young lady who was in no mood for trifling.

"I shall have much pleasure, Miss Strong, in getting it out. What seem to be well-founded rumours have reached England that gold has been found at last in considerable quantities. The shares have gone up with a rush. When the Stock Exchange closed this afternoon they were quoted at £12 10s. A little more than a week ago they were unsaleable at twopence each."

"£12 10s.! oh, Mr. Franklyn! And has Cyril got rid of his?"

"Not a bit of it. They are in my strongbox. There are ten thousand of them—Cyril is one of the largest holders, if he is not the largest; and what that means at £12 10s. apiece you can calculate as well as I."

"Oh, Mr. Franklyn!" The young lady brought her hands together with a little clap. She turned in natural triumph towards her friend. "What did I tell you? Now aren't you sorry for what you said last night? Didn't I say that you hadn't the faintest notion of what you were talking about?"

Miss Wentworth, though, as was to be expected, not so excited as the lady who was principally concerned, evinced sufficiently lively signs of interest.

"You certainly did, and I certainly hadn't; and while you left nothing unsaid which you ought to have said, there can be no sort of doubt whatever that I said everything which I ought to have left unsaid. But, at the same time, I do beg leave to remark that Mr. Paxton need not have worn such an air of mystery."

"Why?" Miss Strong tapped the toe of her slipper against the floor. "He wasn't compelled to blurt out his affairs to all the world."

Miss Wentworth shrugged her shoulders.

"Certainly not—if I am all the world. Are you also all the world? From what I gathered he did not make much of a confidante of you."

"Well, he wasn't forced to!" Suddenly Miss Strong made a wholly irrational, but not wholly unnatural, movement in the direction of Miss Wentworth's chair. She placed her hand upon that lady's shoulders. And she kissed her twice, first on the lips, then on the brow. And she exclaimed, "Never mind. I forgive you!"

Miss Wentworth was quite as demure as the occasion required. She surveyed her emotional friend with twinkling eyes.

"Thank you very much indeed, my dear."

Miss Strong moved restlessly about the room, passing, as it seemed, aimlessly from object to object.

"It is strange that he should have kept such news to himself! And not have said a word about it! And now not coming after all!" She turned to Mr. Franklyn. "I suppose that it is all quite true? That you have not been building up my hopes simply to dash them down again?"

"I have given you an accurate statement of the actual position of affairs when prices were made up for the day, as you may easily prove yourself by a reference to an evening paper."

With her hands Miss Strong pushed back her hair from her temples.

"After all he had lost in Eries—"

Mr. Franklyn interposed a question.

"In Eries! Did he lose in Eries?"

"I am afraid he did, heavily. And then, in spite of that, on the same day, to see his way to a quarter of a million!"

"A quarter of a million! Did he mention that precise amount?"

"I think he did,—I feel sure he did. Charlie, didn't you hear him speak of a quarter of a million?"

Miss Wentworth, who from the depths of her easy chair had been regarding the two almost as if they had been studies of interesting, though contrasting, types of human nature, smiled as she replied—

"I believe that I did hear Mr. Paxton make a passing and, as it seemed to me, a mysterious allusion to that insignificant sum."

"Then he must be acquainted with the movements of the markets." Mr. Franklyn was the speaker. "Though I must tell you candidly, Miss Strong, that at present I am very far from being prepared to advise him to hold until his profits reach what Miss Wentworth, in a truly liberal spirit, calls that insignificant sum. As things stand, he can get out with half of it. If he waits for more, he may get nothing. Indeed, it is an almost vital necessity of the situation that I should see him at once. The shares are in my keeping. Without his direct authority I can do nothing with them. After all, the boom may be but a bubble; it may already have been blown to a bursting-point; in the morning it may have been pricked. Such things are the commonplaces of the Stock Exchange. In any case, it is absolutely necessary that he should be on the spot, ready, if needful, to take prompt, instant advantage of the turn of the market in whatever direction it may be. Or, by the time that he does appear upon the scene, his shares may again be unsaleable at twopence apiece, and all his profits may have gone. Now, tell me, do you know where he stayed last night?"

"At Makell's Hotel. He nearly always does stay there when he is in Brighton."

"It is possible, then, that he is there now; or, at any rate, that they have news of him. I will go at once and inquire."

Miss Strong made a quick movement towards the speaker.

"Mr. Franklyn, mayn't I come with you?"

He hesitated.

"There is not the slightest necessity. If he is there I will bring him back with me; if he is not I will either bring or send you news."

"You promise?"

"I do—certainly."

"You promise that you will let me hear as soon as you can—at once—without a moment's delay?" The girl put her hand to her side. Tears came into her eyes. "Mr. Franklyn, you don't know what all this means to me. All day long I have been conscious of something hanging over me, as it were, a cloud of catastrophe. That something very strange either has happened, or shortly will happen, I am convinced. It frightens me! So, if you wish to do me a kindness, you will not keep me in suspense one moment longer than you can help."

Miss Strong had passed, so far as appearances went, instantly, without any sort of warning, from a white heat of excitement to almost preternatural coldness. One had only to look at her to perceive that her mind was not at ease; nor, since mental and physical conditions are closely allied, her body either. Mr. Franklyn proffered reassurance.

"Believe me, Miss Strong, there is not the slightest real cause for anxiety. The probability is that Cyril is looking for me, just as I am looking for him; that, in fact, we are chasing each other. Anyhow, you shall have news when I have news, and that without a second's delay. I ought to find a cab upon the nearest stand. If I do, you ought to hear from me in thirty minutes. But even if I don't, I think that I can promise that you shall hear from me within the hour."

CHAPTER XI

JOHN IRELAND'S WARRANT

Mr. Franklyn was unable to find a cab. He walked. And as he walked he wondered. Mr. Paxton's conduct seemed to him to be stranger than, in the presence of Miss Strong, he had cared to admit. It was unlike Cyril to have allowed so amazing a change to have taken place in a holding in which he was so largely interested, and yet to have held his peace. Mr. Franklyn had made more considerable efforts to place himself in communication with Cyril than he had hinted at. There had been several things lately in that gentleman's conduct which had struck him as peculiar. But all his efforts had been vain. It was only by chance that that afternoon he had run across an acquaintance who informed him that he had just seen Mr. Paxton leaving Victoria in a Brighton train. Taking it for granted that he was journeying towards Miss Strong, as soon as he could, Franklyn followed on his heels.

And now Miss Strong had seen nothing of him! Indeed, she had been told that he intended to spend the night in town. Coupled with other circumstances, to Mr. Franklyn the thing seemed distinctly odd.

Arrived at Makell's Hotel, he accosted the porter who held the door open for him to enter.

"Is Mr. Paxton staying here?"

"Mr. Paxton is out."

"Out? Then he is staying here?"

"He has been here. I don't know if he is returning. You had better inquire at the office."

Mr. Franklyn inquired. At the office their acquaintance with Mr. Paxton's movements did not appear to be much greater than the porter's. He was out. He might return. He probably would. When, they could not say.

"How long ago is it since he went out?"

"Something over an hour."

"Did he say anything about where he was going to?"

"Not to me. I know nothing, it's only what I surmise, but he went hurrying out as if he had an appointment which he wanted to keep."

"An appointment? Something over an hour ago? Yes, he had an appointment about that time, but he never kept it." Franklyn looked at his watch. The thirty minutes of which he had spoken to Miss Strong were already nearly past. "Can I have a bed here to-night?"

The clerk said that he could. Franklyn took a card out of his pocket-book. He scribbled on it in pencil—

"I shall be at Medina Villas till eleven. Come at once. They are very anxious to have news of you."

Securing it in an envelope, he handed it to the clerk, instructing him, should Mr. Paxton return before he did, to let him have it at once. Then Mr. Franklyn left the hotel, meaning to walk to the cab rank, which was distant only a few yards, and then drive straight back to Medina Villas.

As he walked along the broad pavement some one stopping him, addressed him by name.

"Is that you, Mr. Franklyn?"

The speaker was John Ireland. In his professional capacity as a solicitor Mr. Franklyn had encountered the detective on more than one occasion. The detective's next question took Mr. Franklyn a little by surprise.

"Where's Mr. Paxton?"

Mr. Franklyn looked at his questioner as attentively as the imperfect light would permit. To his trained ear there was something in the inquirer's tone which was peculiar.

"Mr. Paxton! Why do you ask?"

Ireland seemed to hesitate. Then blurted out bluntly—

"Because I've a warrant for his arrest."

Franklyn made a startled movement backwards.

"His arrest! Ireland, you're dreaming!"

"Am I? I'm not of a dreaming sort, as you ought to know by now. Look here, Mr. Franklyn, you and I know each other. I know you're Mr. Paxton's friend, but if you'll take my advice, you won't, for his sake, try to give him a lead away from us. You've just come out of Makell's Hotel. Is he there?"

Mr. Franklyn answered, without pausing a moment for reflection.

"He is not there. Nor did they seem to be able to tell me where he is. I'm quite as anxious to see him as you are."

Ireland slapped his hand against his legs.

"Then I'll be hanged if I don't believe that he's given us the slip. It'll almost serve me right if he has. I ought to have had him without waiting for a warrant, but the responsibility was a bit bigger one than I cared to take. And now some of those pretty friends of his have given him the word, and he's away. If he's clean away, and all because I shirked, I shall almost feel like doing time myself."

When he spoke again Franklyn's manner was caustic.

"Since, Ireland, you appear to wish me to be a little unprofessional, perhaps you also won't mind being a little unprofessional, by way of a quid pro quo. Might I ask you to tell me what is the offence which is specified on the warrant which you say you hold?"

"I don't mind telling you, not the least. In the morning you'll see it for yourself in all the papers—as large as life and twice as natural. Mr. Paxton is wanted for the robbery of the Duchess of Datchet's diamonds."

If the other had struck him Mr. Franklyn could scarcely have seemed more startled.

"The Duchess of Datchet's diamonds! Ireland, are you mad or drunk?"

"Both, if you like. It's as you choose, Mr. Franklyn."

Franklyn eyed the detective as if he really thought that he might be mentally deranged.

"Seriously, Ireland, you don't mean to say that Mr. Paxton—Mr. Cyril Paxton—the Cyril Paxton whom I know—is charged with complicity in the affair of the robbery of the Duchess of Datchet's diamonds?"

"You have hit it, Mr. Franklyn, to a T."

Regardless of the falling drizzle, Mr. Franklyn took off his hat, as if to allow the air a chance to clear his brain.

"But—the thing is too preposterous!—altogether too outrageous for credibility! You yourself must be aware that in the case of a man in Paxton's position, such a step as that which you propose to take is likely to be fraught, for yourself, with the very gravest consequences. And I, on my part, can assure you that you are on the verge of making another of those blunders for which you police are famous. Who is the author of this incredibly monstrous charge?"

"Don't you trouble yourself about that, Mr. Franklyn. People who bring monstrous charges will have to bear the brunt of them. But I tell you what I'll do. You talk about being unprofessional. I'm willing to be a bit more unprofessional for the sake of a little flutter. I'll bet you any reasonable sum you like, at evens, that when we do have him it's proved that at any rate Mr. Paxton knows where the duchess's diamonds are."

"You talk utter nonsense."

"All right, put it so. Anyhow, I'm willing to back my talk. And I'm giving you a chance to back yours."

"Let me understand you. Do you say that you are willing to back your ability to prove that Mr. Paxton has a guilty knowledge of the Datchet diamonds?"

"A guilty knowledge—that's it; you keep on hitting it, and you've hit it again. I'm ready to lay an even hundred pounds—we may as well have something on worth having—that when we do get Mr. Paxton it's proved that he has, as you put it, a guilty knowledge of the whereabouts of the Datchet diamonds."

"Such a supposition is wholly beyond the bounds of reason."

"Will you bet?"

"I will."

"You understand that I'm betting on a certainty; but since you seem to think that you're betting on a certainty too the thing's about even. It's a bet?"

"It is."

"Good! Perhaps you'll make a note of it. I'll make one too." As a matter of fact, Mr. Ireland, taking out his pocket-book, made a note of it upon the spot. "When I've proved my point I'll ask you for that hundred."

"Say, rather, that when you've failed to prove it, I'll ask you."

"All right. And you shall have it, never you fear." Mr. Ireland replaced his pocketbook. "Now I'm going to Makell's to make a few inquiries on my own account. If those inquiries are not satisfactory, I'll at once wire round Mr. Paxton's description. There'll be a reward offered for him in the morning, and if we don't have him within four-and-twenty hours, I'm a Dutchman."

Franklyn, knowing his man, was more moved by Ireland's words than he cared to show.

"For goodness' sake, Ireland, be careful what you do. As you say, you know me, and you know that it is not my custom to express an opinion rashly. I assure you that it is my solemn conviction that if you take the steps which you speak of taking, you will be doing a possibly irreparable injury to a perfectly innocent man."

The detective looked at the lawyer steadily for a second or two.

"Quite right, Mr. Franklyn, I do know you, and it is because I know you that I am willing to strain a point, and, without prejudice to that little bet of ours, give you proof that in matters of this sort a man of my experience is not likely to move without good grounds. You see this?"

Mr. Ireland took something out of his waistcoat pocket. It was a ring. Slipping it on to the tip of his little finger, he held it up for the other to see.

"I see that it's a ring. What of it?"

"As Mr. Paxton was coming out of Makell's Hotel this morning he took his handkerchief out of his pocket. As he did so, unnoticed by him, something dropped out of his handkerchief on to the pavement. It was this ring."

"Well?"

"Ill, I should call it, if I were you, because this ring happens to be one of those which were stolen from the Duchess of Datchet. I had previously had reasons of my own for suspecting that he knew more than was good for him of that business; even you will grant that the discovery in his possession of one of the stolen articles was sufficient to turn suspicion into practical certainty."

Mr. Franklyn said nothing, perhaps because he had nothing to say which he felt was equal to the occasion. What Mr. Ireland said astounded him. He perceived that, at any rate in Mr. Paxton's absence, the position presented the appearance of an aggravating puzzle. That Mr. Paxton could, if he chose, furnish a satisfactory solution, he did not doubt. But he wondered what it was.

The detective went on.

"Now, Mr. Franklyn, since I have been, as you yourself would say, unprofessionally open with you, I must ask you, on your side, to be equally open with me. What are you going to do?"

Franklyn reflected before replying.

"I fail to see how you are entitled to ask me such a question; unless you suspect me also of being an accomplice in the crime. At any rate I decline to answer."

"Very well, Mr. Franklyn, I am sorry, but I must do my duty. I have reason to suspect that you may intend to aid and abet Mr. Paxton in effecting his escape. To prevent your doing so is my obvious duty. Hollier!"

Mr. Ireland beckoned to a man who had hitherto been loitering under the shadow of the houses. Mr. Franklyn might or might not have noticed it, but during their conversation two or three other men had been hanging about within hailing distance in apparently similar purposeless fashion. The individual who had been signalled to approached.

"Mr. Franklyn, this is George Hollier, an officer of police. Hollier, this gentleman's name is Franklyn. He's a friend of Mr. Paxton. I think it's just possible that he will, if he can, give Mr. Paxton a helping hand to get away. I order you to follow him, to observe his movements as closely as you may, and if he does anything which in your judgment looks like an attempt to place himself in communication with Mr. Paxton, to arrest him on the spot. You understand?"

The man nodded. Mr. Franklyn said nothing. He called a cab from the rank in front of them. As the vehicle drew up beside them Mr. Ireland addressed the man upon the box.

"Cabman, what's your number?"

The cabman gave question for question.

"What do you want to know for?"

"I'm an officer of police. This gentleman wishes you to drive him somewhere. It is possible that I may require you to tell me where. You won't lose by it; you needn't be afraid."

The driver gave his number. The detective noted it, as he had done his bet. He called a second cab, again addressing its Jehu.

"Cabman, this man is an officer of police. He's going to ride beside you on the box, and he wants you to keep the cab in which this gentleman is going to be a passenger well in sight. He'll see that you are properly paid for your trouble."

As Mr. Franklyn drove off he was almost tickled by the thought that he, a lawyer of blameless reputation, and of the highest standing, was being followed about the streets of Brighton by a policeman as if he had been a criminal.

But all disposition towards amusement was banished by the further instant reflection that he had promised Miss Strong to bring her news of her lover. And he was bringing her news—of what a character!

CHAPTER XII

A WOMAN ROUSED

Almost as soon as Mr. Franklyn touched the knocker of the house in Medina Villas, the door was opened from within, and he found himself confronted by Miss Strong.

"Oh, Mr. Franklyn, is it you at last?" She saw that some one was standing at Mr. Franklyn's back. "Cyril!" she cried. Then, perceiving her mistake, drew back. "I beg your pardon, I thought it was Mr. Paxton."

The man in the rear advanced.

"Is Mr. Paxton here?" He turned to Mr. Franklyn. "Unless you want trouble, if he is here, you had better tell me."

Mr. Franklyn answered.

"Mr. Paxton is not here. If you like you may go in and look for yourself; but if you are a wise man you will take my assurance as sufficient."

Mr. Hollier looked at Mr. Franklyn, then at Miss Strong, then decided.

"Very well, sir. I don't wish to make myself more disagreeable than I can help. I'll take your word."

Directly he was in the hall and the door was closed Miss Strong caught Mr. Franklyn by the arm. He could feel that she was trembling, as she whispered, almost in his ear—

"Mr. Franklyn, what does that man want with Cyril?"

He drew her with him into the sitting-room. Conscious that he was about to play a principal part in a very delicate situation, he desired to take advantage of still another moment or two to enable him to collect his thoughts. Miss Wentworth, having relinquished her reading, was sitting up in her armchair, awaiting his arrival with an air of evident expectancy. He looked at Miss Strong. Her hand was pressed against her side; her head was thrown a little back; you could see the muscles working in her beautiful, rounded throat almost as plainly as you may see them working in the throat of a bird. For the moment Mr. Franklyn was inclined to wish that Cyril Paxton had never been his friend. He was not a man who was easily unnerved, but as he saw the something which was in the young girl's face, he found himself, for almost the first time in his life, at a loss for words.

Miss Strong had to put her question a second time.

"Mr. Franklyn, what does that man want with Cyril?"

When he did speak the lawyer found, somewhat to his surprise, that his throat seemed dry, and that his voice was husky.

"Strictly speaking, I cannot say that the man wants Cyril at all. What he does want is to know if I am in communication with him."

"Why should he want to know that?" While he was seeking words, Miss Strong followed with another question. "But, tell me, have you seen Cyril?"

"I have not. Though it seems he is in Brighton, or, rather, he was two hours ago."

"Two hours ago? Then where is he now?"

"That at present I cannot tell you. He left his hotel two hours ago, as was thought, to keep an appointment; it would almost seem as if he had been starting to keep the appointment which he had with you."

"Two hours ago? Yes. I was waiting for him then. But he never came. Why didn't he? You know why he didn't. Tell me!"

"The whole affair seems to be rather an odd one, though in all probability it amounts to nothing more than a case of cross-questions and crooked answers. What I have learnt is little enough. If you will sit down I will tell you all there is to tell."

Mr. Franklyn advanced a chair towards Miss Strong with studied carelessness. She spurned the proffered support with something more than contempt.

"I won't sit down. How can I sit down when you have something to tell me? I can always listen best when I am standing."

Putting his hands behind his back, Mr. Franklyn assumed what he possibly intended to be an air of parental authority.

"See here, Miss Strong. You can, if you choose, be as sensible a young woman as I should care to see. If you so choose now, well and good. But I tell you plainly that on your showing the slightest symptom of hysterics my lips will be closed, and you will not get another word out of me."

If by his attempting to play the part of heavy father he had supposed that Miss Strong would immediately be brought into a state of subjection, he had seldom made a greater error. So far from having cowed her, he seemed to have fired all the blood in her veins. She drew herself up until she had increased her stature by at least an inch, and she addressed the man of law in a strain in which he probably had never been addressed before.

"How dare you dictate how I am to receive any scraps of information which you may condescend to dole out to me! You forget yourself. Cyril is to be my husband; you pretend to be his friend. If it is anything but pretence, and you are a gentlemen, and a man of honour, you will see that it is your duty to withhold no tidings of my promised husband from his future wife. How I choose to receive those tidings is my affair, not yours."

Certainly the lady's slightly illogical indignation made her look supremely lovely. Mr. Franklyn recognised this fact with a sensation which was both novel and curious. Even in that moment of perturbation, he told himself that it would never be his fate to have such a beautiful creature breathing burning words for love of him. While he wondered what to answer, Miss Wentworth interposed, rising from her chair to do so.

"Daisy is quite right, Mr. Franklyn. Don't play the game which the cat plays with the mouse by making lumbering attempts to, what is called, break it gently. If you have bad news, tell it out like a man! You will find that the feminine is not necessarily far behind the masculine animal in fibre."

Mr. Franklyn looked from one young woman to the other, and felt himself ill-used. He had known them both for quite a tale of years; and yet he felt, somehow, as if he were becoming really acquainted with them for the first time now.

"You misjudge me, Miss Strong, and you, Miss Wentworth, too. The difficulty which I feel is how to tell you, as we lawyers say, without prejudice, exactly what there is to tell. As I said, the situation is such an odd one. I must begin by asking you a question. Has either of you heard of the affair of the robbery of the Duchess of Datchet's diamonds?"

"The affair of the robbery of the Duchess of Datchet's diamonds?"

Miss Strong repeated his words, passing her hand over her eyes, as if she did not understand. Miss Wentworth, however, made it quickly plain that she did.

"I have; and so of course has Daisy. What of it?"

"This. An addle-headed detective, named John Ireland, has got hold of a wild idea that Cyril knows something about it."

Miss Wentworth gave utterance to what sounded like a half-stifled exclamation.

"I guessed as much! What an extraordinary thing! I had been reading about it just before Mr. Paxton came in last night, and when he began talking in a mysterious way about his having made a quarter of a million at a single coup—precisely the amount at which the diamonds were valued—it set me thinking. I suppose I was a fool."

For Miss Wentworth's quickness in guessing his meaning Mr. Franklyn had been unprepared. If she, inspired solely by the evidence of her own intuitions, had suspected Mr. Paxton, what sort of a case might not Mr. Ireland have against him? But Miss Strong's sense of perception was, apparently, not so keen. She looked at her companions as a person might look who is groping for the key of a riddle.

"I daresay I am stupid. I did read something about some diamonds being stolen. But—what has that to do with Cyril?"

Mr. Franklyn glanced at Miss Wentworth as if he thought that she might answer. But she refrained. He had to speak.

"In all probability the whole affair is a blunder of Ireland's."

"Ireland? Who is Ireland?"

"John Ireland is a Scotland Yard detective, and, like all such gentry, quick to jump at erroneous conclusions."

They saw that Miss Strong made a little convulsive movement with her hands. She clenched her fists. She spoke in a low, clear, even tone of voice.

"I see. And does John Ireland think that Cyril Paxton stole the Datchet diamonds?"

"I fancy that he hardly goes as far as that. From what I was able to gather, he merely suspects him of being acquainted with their present whereabouts."

Although Miss Strong did not raise her voice, it rang with scorn.

"I see. He merely suspects him of that. What self-restraint he shows! And is that John Ireland on the doorstep?"

"That is a man named Hollier, whom John Ireland was good enough to commission to keep an eye on me."

"Why on you? Does he suspect you also?"

Mr. Franklyn shrugged his shoulders.

"He knows that I am Cyril's friend."

"And all Cyril's friends are to be watched and spied upon? I see. And is Cyril arrested? Is he in prison? Is that the meaning of his absence?"

"Not a bit of it. He seems, temporarily, to have disappeared."

"And when he reappears I suppose John Ireland will arrest him?"

"Candidly, Miss Strong, I fear he will."

"There is something else you fear. And which you fear too!"

Miss Strong swung round towards Miss Wentworth with an imperious gesture. Her rage, despite it being tinged with melodrama, was in its way sublime. The young lady's astonishing intensity so carried away her hearers that they probably omitted to notice that there was any connection between her words and manner and the words and manner of, say, the transpontine drama.

"You fear, both of you, that what John Ireland suspects is true. You feel that Cyril Paxton, the man I love, who would not suffer himself to come into contact with dishonour, whose shoestrings you are neither of you worthy to unloose—you fear that he may have soiled his hands with sordid crime. I see your fear branded on your faces—looking from your eyes. You cravens! You cowards! You unutterable things! To dare so to prejudge a man who, as yet, has had no opportunity to know even what it is with which you charge him!"

Suddenly Miss Strong devoted her particular attention to Miss Wentworth. She pointed her words with a force and a directness which ensured their striking home.

"As for you, now I know what it was you meant last night; what it was which in your heart you accused him of, but which your tongue did not dare to quite bring itself to utter. And you have pretended to be my friend, and yet you are so swift to seek to kill that which you know is dearer than life to the man whom I love and hold in honour. Since your friendship is plainly more dangerous than your enmity, in the future we'll be enemies, openly, avowedly, for never again I'll call you friend of mine!"

Miss Wentworth moved forward, exclaiming—

"Daisy!"

But Miss Strong moved back.

"Don't speak to me! Don't come near to me! If you touch me, woman though I am, and woman though you are, I will strike you!"

Since Miss Strong seemed to mean exactly what she said, Miss Wentworth, deeming, under certain given circumstances, discretion to be the better part of valour, held her peace. Miss Strong, having annihilated Miss Wentworth, one could but hope to her entire satisfaction, redirected her attention to the gentleman.

"And you pretended to be Cyril's friend! Heaven indeed preserve us from our friends, it is they who strike the bitterest blows! This only I will say to you. You have the courage of your opinions when there's no courage wanted, but were Cyril Paxton this moment to enter the room you would no more dare to hint to him what you have dared to hint to me, than you would dare to fly."

Then, recollecting herself, with exquisite sarcasm Miss Strong apologised for having confused her meaning.

"I beg your pardon, Mr. Franklyn, a thousand times. I said exactly the contrary of what I wished to say. Of course, if Cyril did enter the room, there is only one thing which you would dare to do, dare to fly. I leave you alone together, in the complete assurance that I am leaving you to enjoy the perfect communion of two equal minds."

Miss Strong moved towards the door. Mr. Franklyn interposed.

"One moment, Miss Strong. Where are you going?"

"To look for Cyril. Do you object? I will try to induce him not to hurt you, when I find him."

"You understand that you will have to endure the ignominy of having the man outside following you wherever you may go."

"Ignominy, you call it! Why, the man may actually be to me as a protection from my friends."

"You use hard words. I enter into your feelings sufficiently to understand that, from your own point of view, they may not seem to be unjustified. But at the same time I am sufficiently your friend, and Cyril's friend, to decline to allow you, if I can help it, to throw dust in your own eyes. That Cyril has been guilty of actual theft, I do not for a moment believe. That he may have perpetrated some egregious blunder, I fear is possible. I know him probably as well as you do. I know John Ireland too, and I am persuaded that he would not bring a charge of this kind without having good grounds to go upon. Indeed, I may tell you plainly—slurring over the truth will do no good to any one—Cyril is known to have been in actual possession of one of the missing jewels."

"I don't believe it."

"Best assured you will do good neither to Cyril's cause nor to your own by a refusal to give credence to actual facts. It is only facts which a judge and jury can be induced to act upon. Satisfactorily explain them if you can, but do not suppose that you will be able to impress other people with the merits of your cause by declining to believe in their existence. I do entreat you to be advised by me before, by some rash, if well-meaning act, you do incalculable mischief to Cyril and yourself."

"Thank you, Mr. Franklyn, but one does not always wish to be advised even by one's legal adviser. Just now I should be obliged by your confining yourself to answering questions. Perhaps you will be so good as to tell me where I am most likely to find John Ireland, that immaculate policeman?"

"When I left him he was just going to Makell's Hotel to make inquiries as to Cyril's whereabouts upon his own account."

"Then I will go to Makell's Hotel to make inquiries of John Ireland upon my account."

"In that case you must excuse me if I come with you. I warn you again, that if you are not careful you may do Cyril more mischief than you have any notion of."

"I shall come too."

This was Miss Wentworth. Miss Strong bowed.

"If you will, you will. Evidently the man on the doorstep is not likely to serve me as an adequate protection against my friends."

Miss Strong put on her hat and mackintosh in what was probably one of the shortest times on record. Miss Wentworth generally dressed more quickly than her friend; on such an occasion she was not likely to be left behind. The curious procession of three passed through the door and down the steps in Indian file, Miss Strong first, Mr. Franklyn last.

At the bottom of the steps stood Mr. Hollier. The leader looked him up and down.

"Is your name Hollier?"

The man touched his hat.

"That's my name, miss."

"I am Daisy Strong, Mr. Cyril Paxton's promised wife." She seemed on a sudden to be fond of advertising the fact. "I am going to look for Mr. Paxton now. You may, if you choose, play the part of spy, and follow me; but let me tell you that if he comes to harm through you, or through any of your associates, there'll be trouble."

"I see, miss."

Mr. Hollier grinned, hurting, as it seemed, the lady's sense of dignity.

"I don't know what you see to smile at. A woman has given a man sufficient cause for tears before to-day. You may find, in your own case, that she will again."

CHAPTER XIII

THE DETECTIVE AND THE LADY

Mr. Ireland marched into Makell's Hotel as if he owned the building. He created a sensation in the office.

"You know me?"

The clerk, who was a good-looking young gentleman, with a curled moustache, eyed the speaker with somewhat supercilious curiosity. Mr. Ireland's manner was more suggestive of his importance than was his appearance. The clerk decided that he did not know him. He owned as much.

"I'm Inspector Ireland, of the Criminal Investigation Department. I hold a warrant for the arrest of Cyril Paxton. He is stopping in your hotel. I don't want to cause any more trouble than necessary—my assistants are outside—so, perhaps, you will tell me whereabouts in the house I am likely to find him."

The clerk looked the surprise which he felt.

"Mr. Paxton is out."

"Are you sure?"

"I will make inquiries if you wish it. But I know that he is out. I saw him go, and, as I have not left the office since he went, if he had returned I could not have helped seeing him."

"Has he any property here?"

"I will speak to the manager."

The clerk turned as if to suit the action to the word. Reaching through the office window, Mr. Ireland caught him by the shoulder.

"All right. You send for him. I'll speak to him instead."

The clerk eyed the detaining hand with an air of unconcealed disgust.

"Very good. Have the kindness to remove your hand. If you are a policeman, as you say you are, yours is not the kind of grasp which I care to have upon my shoulder."

"Hoity-toity! Don't you injure yourself, young man. All I want is to have the first talk with the manager. Are you going to send for the manager, or am I?"

"Here is the manager."

As the clerk spoke, and before he had had time to properly smooth his ruffled plumes, the dignitary in question entered the office from an inner room. John Ireland accosted him.

"Are you the manager of this hotel—name of Treadwater?"

"I am Mr. Treadwater."

Ireland explained who he was, and what he wanted. Mr. Treadwater was evidently even more surprised than the clerk had been.

"You have a warrant for the arrest of Cyril Paxton! Not our Mr. Paxton, surely?"

"I don't know about your Mr. Paxton; but it's the Mr. Paxton who's stopping here, so don't you make any mistake about it. I'm told he's out. One of my men will stay here till he returns. In the meantime I want to know if there is any property of his about the place. If there is, I want to have a look at it."

The manager considered.

"I don't wish to seem to doubt, Mr. Ireland, that you are what you say you are, or, indeed, anything at all that you have said. But an effort has already been made once to-day to gain access—under what turned out to be false pretences—to certain property which Mr. Paxton has committed to our keeping. And I am compelled to inform you that it is a rule of ours not, under any circumstances, to give up property which has been intrusted to us by our guests to strangers without a proper authority."

Ireland smiled grimly.

"Where is there somewhere I can speak to you in private? I'll show you authority enough, and to spare."

The manager, having taken Mr. Ireland into the inner room, the detective lost no time in explaining the position.

"You're a sensible man, Mr. Treadwater. You don't want to have any bother in a place of this sort, and I don't want to make any more bother than I'm compelled. Mr. Paxton's wanted for a big thing, about as big a thing as I've ever been engaged in. I wasn't likely to come here without my proper credentials, hardly. Just you cast your eye over this."

Ireland unfolded a blue paper which he had taken from among a sheaf of other papers, which were in the inner pocket of his coat, and held it up before the manager's face.

"That's a search warrant. If you're not satisfied with what you see of it, I'll read it to you, and that's all I'm bound to do. I've reason to believe that Cyril Paxton has certain stolen property in his possession here, in this hotel. If you choose to give me facilities to examine any property he may have, well and good. If you don't choose, this warrant authorises me to search the building. I'll call my men in, and I'll have it searched from attic to basement—every drawer and every box which the place contains, if it takes us all night to do it."

Mr. Treadwater rubbed his hands together. He did not look pleased.

"I had no idea, when I spoke, that you were in possession of such a document. As you say, I certainly do not wish to have a bother. A search warrant is authority enough, even for me. All the property Mr. Paxton has in the hotel is in this room. I will show it to you." The manager moved to a door which seemed to have been let into the wall. "This is our strong-room. As you perceive, it is a letter lock. Only one person, except myself, ever has the key to it."

While he was speaking he opened the door. He disappeared into the recess which the opening of the door disclosed. Presently he reappeared carrying a Gladstone in his hand. He laid the bag on the table, in front of Mr. Ireland.

"That is all the property Mr. Paxton has in the hotel."

"How do you know?"

The manager smiled—the smile of superiority.

"My dear sir, it is part of my duty to know what every guest brings into the hotel. You can, if you like, go up to the room which he occupied last night, but you'll find nothing in it of Mr. Paxton's. All that he brought with him is contained in that Gladstone bag."

"Then we'll see what's in it. I'm going to open it in your presence, so that you'll be evidence to prove that I play no hankey-pankey tricks."

Mr. Ireland did open it in the manager's presence. With, considering the absence of proper tools, a degree of dexterity which did him credit. But after all it appeared that there was nothing in it to adequately reward him for the trouble he had taken. The bag was filled chiefly with shirts and underclothing. Although every article seemed to be bran-new, there was absolutely nothing which, correctly speaking, could be said to be of value. With total want of ceremony the investigator turned the entire contents of the bag out upon the table. But though he did so, nothing in any way out of the common was discovered.

Judging from the expression of his countenance, Mr. Ireland did not seem to be contented.

"Wasn't there an attempt at burglary here last night? One's been reported."

"There was. For the first time in the history of the hotel. An attempt was made from the street to gain admission through the window, to Mr. Paxton's bedroom."

"And didn't you say that an attempt had been made to-day to gain access, by means of false pretences, to Mr. Paxton's property?"

"That is so."

"And didn't he ask you to keep that property safe in your strong-room?"

"He did."

"Well—doesn't it seem as if somebody was precious anxious to lay his hands upon that property, and that Mr. Paxton was equally anxious that he shouldn't?"

"Precisely."

"And yet you go and tell me that all the property he has is contained in that Gladstone bag. What is there that should make any one go out of his way to take it? You tell me that!"

When the manager replied, it was with an appreciable amount of hesitation.

"I think that is a point on which I may be able to throw some light."

"Then throw it—do!"

"I shouldn't be surprised if Mr. Paxton took all that the bag contained which was of value up to London with him this morning, and left it there. Indeed, this evening, before he went out, he told me that that was what he had done."

Mr. Ireland gave utterance to what, coming from the mouth of any one but an inspector of police, would have sounded like a string of execrations.

"I suppose you've no idea what it was that he took with him or where it was he took it?"

"Not the faintest notion."

"Mr. Treadwater, this is another illustration of the fact that if you want a thing well done you must do it yourself. This morning I set a man to shadow Mr. Paxton—I told him not to let him get out of his sight. What does he do, this utter idiot? He sees our gentleman drop a ring. My man, he picks it up, and he gets into such a state of excitement that he loses his head and tears straight off with it to me. I'm not saying that he'd not chanced upon an important piece of evidence, because he had; but if he'd kept his wits about him, and had his head screwed on straight, he'd have had the ring and Mr. Paxton too. As it was, that was the last he saw of Mr. Paxton."

"May I ask what it is you suspect Mr. Paxton of having taken with him up to town?"

"Unless I'm out of my reckoning, Mr. Paxton went up to town with the Duchess of Datchet's diamonds stowed away in his pockets."

The manager's face was a vivid note of exclamation.

"No! My dear sir, I have been acquainted with Mr. Paxton some considerable time. I happen to know that he's a gentleman of position in the City. You must surely be mistaken in supposing that he could be mixed up in such an affair as that—it's incredible!"

"Is it? That's all right. If you like, you think so. Gentlemen of position in the City have had their fingers in some queer pies before to-day. If you don't happen to know it, I present you with the information gratis. Have you any idea of where he was going when he went out to-night?"

"I fancy that when he comes to Brighton he comes to see a lady. I rather took it for granted that, as usual, he was going to her."

"What's her name; and where does she live?"

"I don't know her name; but I believe she lives in Medina Villas—that, you know, is at West Brighton."

"Medina Villas?" Ireland seemed to be turning something over in his mind. He smiled. "I shouldn't be surprised. If she does, I'm inclined to think that one of my men has got his eye on her address. If Mr. Paxton's there, he's nabbed. But I'm afraid he isn't. On this occasion I'm inclined to think that he had an appointment which he found to be slightly more pressing than that which he had with the lady." Ireland looked at the manager with what he probably intended for a look of frankness. "I don't mind owning that there are features about the case, as it stands at present, which are beyond my comprehension, and I tell you, I would give a good round sum to be able this moment to lay my finger on Mr. Paxton."

"So would I. I'd give a great deal to be able to lay my finger on Mr. Paxton. With all my heart I would. Yes, sir, indeed I would."

Each of the talkers had been too much interested in what the other had to say to notice that while they talked, without invitation or any sort of announcement, a procession—the procession of three!—had entered the room. The speaker was, of course, Miss Strong. Behind her, gripping the handle of her parasol, as it seemed a little nervously, came Miss Wentworth. Mr. Franklyn, looking distinctly the most uncomfortable of the trio, brought up the rear. Miss Strong, in front, bore herself like a female paladin. She held herself quite straight; her shoulders were thrown well back; her dainty head was gallantly poised upon her lovely neck; she breathed the air of battle. She might not have known it, but seldom had she looked more charming. The detective and the manager both looked at her askance. She only looked at the detective.

"Are you John Ireland?"

"I am. Though I have not the pleasure, madam, of knowing you."

"I am Daisy Strong, who am shortly to be Cyril Paxton's wife. How dare you, Mr. Ireland, so foully slander him!"

Mr. Ireland showed symptoms of being surprised. He had an eye for a lady, and still more, perhaps, for a pretty girl. And by neither was he accustomed to being addressed in such a strain.

"I trust, madam, that I have not slandered Mr. Paxton."

"You trust so, do you? Mr. Franklyn, will you come forward, please, instead of hanging behind there in the shadow of Miss Wentworth's skirts, as if you were afraid?"

Mr. Franklyn, thus addressed, came forward, looking, however, as if he would rather not.

"You hear what this person says. And yet you tell me he has slandered Cyril Paxton as foully as he could."

Mr. Franklyn shot a glance at Mr. Ireland which was meant to be pregnant with meaning. He showed a disposition to hum and to ha.

"My dear Miss Strong, I'm sure you will find that Mr. Ireland is not unreasonable. His only desire is to do his duty."

Miss Strong stamped her foot upon the floor.

"His duty! to slander a gentleman in whose presence he is not worthy to stand! Because a man calls himself a policeman, and by doubtful methods contrives to earn the money with which to keep himself alive, is such an one entitled to fling mud at men of stainless honour and untarnished reputation, and then to excuse himself by pretending that flinging mud is his duty? If you, Mr. Franklyn, are afraid of a policeman, merely because he's a policeman, I assure you I am not. And I take leave to tell Mr. Ireland that there are policemen who are, at least, as much in want of being kept in order as any member of the criminal classes by any possibility could be."

Ireland eyed the eloquent lady as if he were half-puzzled, half-amused.

"I understand your feelings, madam, and I admire your pluck in standing up for Mr. Paxton."

Again the lady stamped her foot.

"I care nothing for your approval! And it has nothing at all to do with the matter on hand."

The detective coughed apologetically.

"Perfectly true, madam. But I can't help it. I assure you I always do admire a young woman who sticks up for her young man when he happens to find himself in a bit of a scrape. But, if you take my tip, Miss Strong, you'll leave us men to manage these sort of things. You'll only do Mr. Paxton harm by interfering. You tell her, Mr. Franklyn, if what I say isn't true."

Miss Strong turned towards Mr. Ireland, cutting short the words on Franklyn's lips before they had a chance of getting themselves spoken.

"Do not refer to Mr. Franklyn on any matter which concerns me. There is no connection between us. Mr. Franklyn and I are strangers. I am quite capable of taking care of myself. I even think that you may find me almost a match for you." She turned to Treadwater. "Is Mr. Paxton stopping in this hotel?"

"He stayed here last night, madam. And he has been here again this evening. At present, he is out."

"And what is this?"

She motioned towards the open bag, with its contents strewed upon the table.

"That is Mr. Paxton's. Mr. Ireland has forced it open."

Miss Strong turned towards Ireland—a veritable feminine fury.

"You wretched spy! you cowardly thief! To take advantage of a man's back being turned to poke and pry among his private possessions in order to gratify your curiosity! Is that the science of detection?" She transferred her attentions to the manager. "And you—are those the lines on which your hotel is conducted, that you hand over, in their absence, the belongings of your guests to the tender mercies of such a man as this? If so, then your methods of management ought to be known more widely than they are. Decent people will then know what they have to expect when they trust themselves inside your doors."

Treadwater did not seem as if he altogether relished the fashion of the lady's speech. He began to make excuses.

"I protested against Mr. Ireland's action; but on his producing a search warrant, I yielded to the pressure of necessity."

"The pressure of necessity! Do you call this the pressure of necessity?"

Miss Strong pointed a scornful finger at Mr. Ireland. Ostentatiously ignoring her, the detective addressed himself to the manager.

"I'm going now, Mr. Treadwater. I'll leave one of my men behind me. If Mr. Paxton returns, he'll deal with him."

The lady interposed.

"What do you mean—he'll deal with him?"

"What do I mean? I mean that Mr. Paxton will be arrested as soon as he shows his nose inside the door. And I'll tell you what, Miss Strong, if you were to use fewer hard words, and were to do something to prove Mr. Paxton's innocence, instead of talking big about it, you might do him more good than you're likely to do by the way in which you've been going on up to now. I'll put these things together and take them with me."

By "these things" Mr. Ireland meant Mr. Paxton's. He moved towards the table. Miss Strong thrust herself between him and it.

"Don't touch them—don't dare to touch them! Don't dare to touch Cyril's property! Do you suppose that, because you're a policeman, all the world can be cowed into suffering you to commit open robbery?"

She clutched at the table with both her hands, glaring at him like some wild cat. Shrugging his shoulders, Ireland laughed, shortly, grimly.

"Very good, Miss Strong. There is nothing there which is of the slightest consequence in this particular case. You are welcome to take them in your custody. Only, remember, you assume the responsibility for their safe keeping."

"The man who forces open another man's portmanteau without the knowledge of its owner becomes, I fancy, at once responsible for its contents. And I promise you that if the slightest article is missing you will be taught that even a policeman can be called to account."

Without attempting to answer her, Ireland went towards the door, pausing, as he went, to whisper to Mr. Franklyn—

"Why did you bring her with you? She'll only make bad worse."

Mr. Franklyn shrugged his shoulders, as the detective himself had done.

"I didn't bring her! She brought me!"

Miss Strong's clear tones came after the detective.

"You set a man to spy on me, Mr. Ireland, and now I mean to spy on you. We'll see if turn and turn about is not fair play, and if you dare to try to prevent my going exactly where I please."

Still ignoring her, Ireland went into the hall. There he found Hollier in waiting.

"Any report, Hollier?"

"Nothing material, sir. I followed Mr. Franklyn to Medina Villas and back, but saw nothing to cause me to suppose that he was in communication with Mr. Paxton."

"You remain here until I relieve you. If Mr. Paxton returns, arrest him. Send for me if I am required. I will leave a man outside, so that you can have help, if it is needed."

Ireland went through the hall, and through the door, Miss Strong hard upon his heels. On the steps he turned and spoke to her.

"Now, Miss Strong, if you are wise, you'll go home and go to bed. You may do as you like about attempting to follow me, but I promise you, I shall not permit you to dog my footsteps one moment longer than it suits my convenience. On that point you need be under no misapprehension."

The detective strode away. Miss Strong was about to follow, when Miss Wentworth caught her by the arm.

"Now, Daisy, be reasonable—you'll do no good by persisting—let's go home."

"Loose my arm."

Miss Wentworth loosed it.

In less than a minute Daisy had decreased the distance between Ireland and herself to half a dozen feet. Franklyn and Miss Wentworth came after, splashing through the mud and the mist, somewhat disconsolately, a few paces in the rear.

The cavalcade had gone, perhaps, fifty yards, when a figure, dashing out of an entry they were passing, caught Ireland by the lapel of his sleeve.

"Guv'nor! I want to speak to you!"

The figure was that of a man—an undersized, half-grown, very shabby-looking man. The light was not bad enough to conceal so much. The collar of a ragged, dirty coat was turned up high about his neck, and an ancient billycock was crammed down upon his head. Stopping, Ireland turned and looked at him.

"You want to speak to me?"

"Yes, Mr. Ireland; don't yer know me?"

"Know you?" Suddenly Ireland's arm went out straight from the shoulder, and the stranger, as if he had been a rat, was gripped tightly by the neck. "Yes, Bill Cooper, I do know you. I've been looking for you some time. There's something which I rather wish to say to you. Now, what's your little game?"

The man's voice became a whine; the change was almost excusable when one considers how uncomfortable he must have been in the detective's grasp. Daisy, who was standing within a yard, could hear distinctly every word that was uttered.

"Don't be nasty, Mr. Ireland, that ain't like you! I know you want me—that's all right—but if you take me without hearing what I've got to say you'll be sorry all the same."

"Sorry, shall I? How do you make that out?"

"Why, because I'll make your fortune for you if you'll give me half a chance—leastways, I daresay it's made already, but I'll double it for you, anyhow."

"And pray how do you propose to do that?"

"Why, I'll put you on to the biggest thing that ever you were put on to."

"You mean that you'll round on your comrades. I see. Is that it?"

The stranger did not seem to altogether like the fashion in which Mr. Ireland summed up his intentions.

"You may call it what you please, but if I hadn't been used bad first of all myself, I wouldn't have said a word; red-hot irons wouldn't have made me. But when a chap's been used like I've been used, he feels like giving of a bit of it back again; that's fair enough, ain't it?"

"Chuck the patter, Bill. Go on with what you have to say."

"Look here, Mr. Ireland, you give me ten thick 'uns, enough to take me to 'Merriker; I'll go there, and I'll put you on to them as had something to do with them there Duchess of Datchet's diamonds what's been and got theirselves mislaid."

It was Daisy who answered. She seemed to speak in sudden and uncontrollable excitement. "I don't know what ten thick 'uns are, but if you do what you say I'll give you fifty pounds out of my own pocket."

The man regarded Miss Strong with an inquiring eye.

"I don't know you, miss. Mr. Ireland, who's the lady?"

"The lady's all right. She's a bit interested in the Datchet diamonds herself. If she says she'll give you fifty pounds you'll get 'em, only you've got to earn 'em, mind!"

"Fifty pound!" The man drew a long breath.

"I'd do pretty nigh anything for fifty pound, let alone the way they've been and used me. I've been having a cruel hard time, I have—cruel hard!"

Ireland took Cooper by the shoulder and shook him, with the apparent intention of waking him up.

"All right, Mr. Ireland, all right; there ain't no call for you to go handling of me; I ain't doing nothing to you. I don't know the lady, and she don't know me, and I'm only a-trying to see that's it's all right. You wouldn't do a pore bloke, miss, would you? That fifty'll be all right?"

Mr. Ireland presented Cooper with a second application of the previous dose.

"That fifty'll be all right, or rather it'll be all wrong, if you keep me standing here much longer in the rain."

"You are so hasty, Mr. Ireland, upon my word you are. I'm a-coming to it, ain't I? Now I'll tell you straight. Tom the Toff, he done the nicking; and the Baron, he put him up to it." Miss Strong looked bewildered.

"Tom the Toff? The Baron? Who are they?"

The detective spoke.

"I know who they are, Miss Strong. And I may tell Mr. Cooper that I've had an eye on those two gentlemen already. What I want to know is where the diamonds are. They're worth more than the rogues who took them. Now, Bill, where are the shiners?"

Cooper stretched out both his hands in front of him with a gesture which was possibly intended to impress Mr. Ireland with a conviction of his childlike candour.

"That's where it is—just exactly where it is! I don't know where the shiners are—and that's the trewth! Yet more don't nobody else seem to know where the shiners are! That's what the row's about! Seems as how the shiners has hooked theirselves clean off—and ain't there ructions! So far as I can make out from what I've come across and put together, don't yer know, it seems as how a cove as they calls Paxton—"

"Paxton!"

The name came simultaneously from Ireland and Miss Strong.

"I don't know as that's his name—that's only what I've heard 'em call him, don't yer know. He's a rare fine toff, a regular out-and-outer, whatever his name is. It seems as how this here cove as they calls Paxton has been playing it off on the Toff and the Baron, and taken the whole blooming lot of sparklers for his own—so far as I can make out, he has."

"It's a lie!"

This was, of course, Miss Strong. The plain speaking did not seem to hurt Mr. Cooper's feelings.

"That I don't know nothing at all about; I'm only telling you what I know. And I do know that they've had a go at this here cove as they calls Paxton more than once, and more than twice, and that now they've got him fast enough."

Mr. Ireland twisted Cooper round, so that the electric lamplight shone on his face.

"What do you mean—they've got him fast enough?"

"I mean what I says, don't I? They got hold of him this evening, and they've took him to a crib they got, and if he don't hand over them sparklers they'll murder him as soon as look at him."

Miss Strong turned to the detective with shining eyes.

"Mr. Ireland, save him! What shall we do?"

"Don't put yourself out, Miss Strong. This may turn out to be the best thing that could have happened to Mr. Paxton. Bill, where's this crib of theirs?"

Cooper pushed his hat on to the side of his head.

"I don't know as how I could rightly describe it to you—Brighton ain't my home, you know. But I daresay I could show it to you if I was to try."

"Then you shall try. Listen to me, Bill Cooper. If you take me to this crib of theirs, and if what you say is true, and you don't try to play any of those tricks of yours, I'll add something of my own to this lady's fifty, and it'll be the best stroke of business that you ever did in all your life."

Ireland called a cab. He allowed Daisy to enter first. Cooper got in after her.

"The police-station, driver—as fast as you can."

Cooper immediately wanted to get out again.

"Where are you a-taking me to? I ain't going to no police-station!"

"Stay where you are, you idiot! So long as you act fairly with me, I'll act fairly with you. You don't suppose that this is a sort of job that I can tackle single-handed? I'm going to the station to get help. Now then, driver, move that horse of yours!"

The cab moved off, leaving Miss Wentworth and Mr. Franklyn to follow in another if they chose.

CHAPTER XIV

AMONG THIEVES

Cyril was vaguely conscious of the touch of some one's hand about the region of his throat; not of a soft or a gentle hand, but of a clumsy, fumbling, yet resolute paw. Then of something falling on to him— falling with a splashing sound. He opened his eyes, heavily, dreamily. He heard a voice, speaking as if from afar.

"Hullo, chummie, so you ain't dead, after all?—leastways, not as yet you ain't."

The voice was not a musical voice, nor a friendly one. It was harsh and husky, as if the speaker suffered from a chronic cold. It was the voice not only of an uneducated man, but of the lowest type of English-speaking human animal. Cyril shuddered as he heard it. His eyes closed of their own accord.

"Now then!"

The words were accompanied by a smart, stinging blow on Mr. Paxton's cheek, a blow from the open palm of an iron-fronted hand. Severe though it was, Paxton was in such a condition of curious torpor that it scarcely seemed to stir him. It induced him to open his eyes again, and that, apparently, was all.

"Look here, chummie, if you're a-going to make a do of it, make a do of it, and we'll bury you. But if you're going to keep on living, move yourself, and look alive about it. I ain't going to spend all my time waiting for you—it's not quite good enough."

While the flow of words continued, Cyril endeavoured to get the speaker's focus—to resolve his individuality within the circuit of his vision. And, by degrees, it began to dawn on him that the man was, after all, quite close to him: too close, indeed—very much too close. With a sensation of disgust he realised that the fellow's face was actually within a few inches of his own—realised, too, what an unpleasant face it was, and that the man's horrible breath was mingling with his. It was an evil face, the face of one who had grown prematurely old. Staring eyes were set in cavernous sockets. A month's growth of bristles accentuated the animalism of the man's mouth, and jaw, and chin. His ears stuck out like flappers. His forehead receded. His scanty, grizzled hair looked as if it had been shaved off close to his head. Altogether, the man presented a singularly unpleasant picture. As Paxton grasped, slowly enough, how unpleasant, he became conscious of a feeling of unconquerable repulsion.

"Who are you?" he asked.

His voice did not sound to him as if it were his own. It was thin, and faint like the voice of some puny child.

"Me?" The fellow chuckled—not by any means in a way which was suggestive of mirth. "I'm the Lord Mayor and Aldermen—that's who I am."

Paxton's senses were so dulled, and he felt so stupid, that he was unable to understand, on the instant, if the fellow was in earnest.

"The Lord Mayor and Aldermen—you?"

The man chuckled again.

"Yes; and likewise the Dook of Northumberland and the Archbishop of Canterbury. Let alone the Queen's own R'yal physician, what's been specially engaged, regardless of all cost, to bring you back to life, so as you can be killed again."

The man's words made Cyril think. Killed again? What had happened to him already? Where was he? Something seemed suddenly to clear his brain, and to make him conscious of the strangeness of his surroundings. He tried to move, and found he could not.

"What's the matter? Where am I?"

"As for what's the matter, why, there's one or two things as is the matter. And, as for where you are, why, that's neither here nor there. If I was you, I wouldn't ask no questions."

Mr. Paxton looked at the speaker keenly. His eyesight was improving. The sense of accurate perception was returning to him fast. The clearer his head became, the more acutely he realised that something beyond the normal seemed to be weighing on his physical frame, and to clog all the muscles of his body.

"What tricks have you been playing on me?"

The man's huge mouth was distorted by a mirthless grin.

"There you are again, asking of your questions. Ain't I told yer, not half a moment since, that if I was you I wouldn't? I've only been having a little game with you, that's all."

The man's tone stirred Paxton to sudden anger. It was all he could do to prevent himself giving utterance to what, under the circumstances, would have been tantamount to a burst of childish petulance. He tried again to move, and immediately became conscious that at least the upper portion of his body was sopping wet, and he was lying in what seemed to be a pool of water.

"What's this I'm lying in?"

For answer the man, taking up a pail which had been standing by his side, dashed its contents full into Cyril's face.

"That's what you're lying in—about eighteen gallons or so of that; as nice clean water as ever you swallowed. You see, I've had to give you a sluicing or two, to liven you up. We didn't want to feel, after all the trouble we've had to get you, as how we'd lost you."

The water, for which Mr. Paxton had been wholly unprepared, and which had been hurled at him with considerable force, had gone right into his eyes and mouth. He had to struggle and gasp for breath. His convulsive efforts seemed to amuse his assailant not a little.

"That's right, choke away! A good plucked one you are, from what I hear. Fond of a bit of a scrap, I'm told. A nice little job they seem to have had of it a-getting of you here."

As the fellow spoke, the events of the night came back to Cyril in a sudden rush of memory. His leaving the hotel, flushed with excitement; the glow of pleasure which had warmed the blood in his veins at the prospect of meeting Daisy laden with good tidings—he remembered it all. Remembered, too, how, when he had scarcely started on his quest, some one, unexpectedly, had come upon him from behind, and how a cloth had been thrown across his face and held tightly against his mouth—a wet cloth, saturated with some sticky, sweet-smelling stuff. And how it had dragged him backwards, overpowering him all at once with a sense of sickening faintness. He had some misty recollection, too, of a cab standing close beside him, and of his being forced into it. But memory carried him no further; the rest was blank.

He had been kidnapped—that was clear enough; the cloth had been soaked with chloroform—that also was sufficiently clear. The after-effects of chloroform explained the uncomfortable feeling which still prostrated him. But by whom had he been kidnapped? and why? and how long ago? and where had his captors brought him?

He was bound hand and foot—that also was plain. His hands were drawn behind his back and tied together at the wrists, with painful tightness, as he was realising better and better every moment. He had been thrown on his back, so that his whole weight lay on his arms. What looked like a clothes line had been passed over his body, fastened to a ring, or something which was beneath him, on the floor, and then drawn so tightly across his chest that not only was it impossible for him to move, but it was even hard for him to breathe. As if such fastenings were not enough, his feet and legs had been laced together and rendered useless, cords having been wound round and round him from his ankles to his thighs. A trussed fowl could not have been more helpless. The wonder was that, confined in such bonds, he had ever been able to escape the stupefying effects of the chloroform—even with the aid of his companion's pail of water.

The room in which he was lying was certainly not an apartment in any modern house. The floor was bare, and, as he was painfully conscious, unpleasantly uneven. The ceiling was low and raftered, and black with smoke. At one end was what resembled a blacksmith's furnace rather than an ordinary stove. Scattered about were not only hammers and other tools, but also a variety of other implements, whose use he did not understand. The place was lighted by the glowing embers of a fire, which smouldered fitfully upon the furnace, and also by a lamp which was suspended from the centre of the raftered ceiling—the glass of which badly needed cleaning. A heavy deal table stood under the lamp, and this, together with a wooden chair and a stool or two, was all the furniture the place contained. How air and ventilation were obtained Paxton was unable to perceive, and the fumes which seemed to escape from the furnace were almost stifling in their pungency.

While Paxton had been endeavouring to collect his scattered senses, so that they might enable him, if possible, to comprehend his situation, the man with the pail had been eyeing him with a curious grin.

Paxton asked himself, as he looked at him, if the man might not be susceptible to the softening influence of a substantial bribe. He decided, at any rate, to see if he had not in his constitution such a thing as a sympathetic spot.

"These ropes are cutting me like knives. If you were to loosen them a bit you would still have me tied as tight as your heart could desire. Suppose you were to ease them a trifle."

The fellow shook his head.

"It couldn't be done, not at no price. It's only a-getting of yer used to what's a-coming—it ain't nothing to what yer going to have, lor' bless yer, no. The Baron, he says to me, says he, 'Tie 'em tight,' he says, 'don't let's 'ave no fooling,' he says. 'So as when the Toff's a-ready to deal with him he'll be in a humbler frame of mind.'"

"The Baron?—the Toff?—who are they?"

"There you are again, a-asking of your questions. If you ask questions I'll give you another dose from this here pail."

The speaker brandished his pail with a gesture which was illustrative of his meaning. Paxton felt, as he regarded him, that he would have given a good round sum to have been able to carry on a conversation with him on terms of something like equality.

"What's your name?"

"What!"

As, almost unconsciously, still another question escaped Mr. Paxton's lips, the fellow, moving forward, brandished his pail at arm's length above his shoulders. Although he expected, momentarily, that the formidable weapon would be brought down with merciless force upon his unprotected face and head, Paxton, looking his assailant steadily in the eyes, showed no signs of flinching. It was, possibly, this which induced the fellow to change his mind—for change it he apparently did. He brought the pail back slowly to its original position.

"Next time you'll get it. I'm dreadful short of temper, I am—can't stand no crossing. Talk to me about the state of the nation, or the price of coals, or your mother-in-law, and I'm with you, but questions I bar."

Paxton tried to summon up a smile.

"Under different circumstances I should be happy to discuss with you the political and other tendencies of the age, but just at present, for conversation on such an exalted plane, the conditions can scarcely be called auspicious."

Up went the pail once more.

"None of your sauce for me, or you'll get it. Now, what's the matter?"

The matter was that Paxton had closed his eyes and compressed his lips, and that a suggestive pallor had come into his cheeks. The pain of his ligatures was rapidly becoming so excruciating that it was as much as he could do to bear it and keep his senses.

"These ropes of yours cut like knives," he murmured.

Instead of being moved to pity, the fellow was moved to smile.

"Like another pailful—hot or cold?"

It was a moment or two before Paxton could trust himself to speak. When he did it was once more with the ghastly semblance of a smile.

"What a pleasant sort of man you seem to be!"

"I am that for certain sure."

"What would you say to a five-pound note?"

"Thank you; I've got one or two of them already. Took 'em out of your pocket, as you didn't seem to have no use for them yourself."

While Paxton was endeavouring, seemingly, to grasp the full meaning of this agreeable piece of information, a door at the further end of the room was opened and some one else came in. Paxton turned his head to see who it was. It was with a sense of shock, and yet, with a consciousness that it was, after all, what he might have expected, that he perceived that the newcomer was the ill-favoured associate of Mr. Lawrence, towards whom he had felt at first sight so strong an aversion. He was attired precisely as he had been when Paxton had seen him last—in the long, loose, black overcoat and the amazingly high tall hat. As he stood peering across the room, he looked like some grotesque familiar spirit come straight from shadowland.

"Well, my Skittles, and is our good friend still alive—eh?"

The man with the pail thus addressed as Skittles grinned at Paxton as he answered.

"The blokey's all right. Him and me's been having a little friendly talk together."

"Is that so? I hope, my Skittles, you have been giving Mr. Paxton a little good advice?"

The man with the curious foreign accent came, and, standing by Cyril's side, glowered down on him like some uncanny creature of evil origin.

"Well, Mr. Paxton, I am very glad to see you, sir, underneath this humble roof—eh?"

Paxton looked up at him as steadily as the pain which he was enduring would permit.

"I don't know your name, sir, or who you are, but I must request you to give me, if you can, an explanation of this extraordinary outrage to which I have been subjected?"

"Outrage—eh? You have been subjected to outrage? Alas! It is hard, Mr. Paxton, that a man of your character should be subjected to outrage—not true—eh?"

"You'll be called to account for this, for that you may take my word. My absence has been discovered long ago, and I have friends who will leave no stone unturned till they have tracked you to your lair."

"Those friends of yours, Mr. Paxton, will be very clever if they track me to what you call my lair until it is too late—for you! You have my promise. Before that time, if you are not very careful, you will be beyond the reach of help."

"At any rate I shall have the pleasure of knowing that, for your share in the transaction, you'll be hanged."

The German-American shrugged his shoulders.

"Well, perhaps. That is likely, anyhow. It is my experience that, sooner or later, one has to pay for one's little amusements, as, Mr. Paxton, you are now to find."

Paxton's lips curled. There was something about the speaker's manner—in his voice, with its continual suggestion of a sneer, about his whole appearance—which filled him with a sense of loathing to which he would have found it impossible to give utterance in words. He felt as one might feel who is brought into involuntary contact with an unclean animal.

"I don't know if you are endeavouring to frighten me. Surely you are aware that I am not to be terrified by threats?"

"With threats? Oh, no! I do not wish to frighten you with threats. That I will make you afraid, is true, but it will not be with threats—I am not so foolish. You think that nothing will make you afraid? Mr. Paxton, I have seen many men like that. When a man is fresh and strong, and can defend himself, and still has hopes, it takes a deal, perhaps, to make him afraid. But when a man is helpless, and is in the hands of those who care not what he suffers, and he has undergone a little course of scientific treatment, there comes a time when he is afraid—oh, yes! As you will see. Why, Mr. Paxton, what is the matter with you? You look as if you were afraid already."

Paxton's eyes were closed, involuntarily. Beads of sweat stood upon his brow. The muscles of his face seemed to be convulsed. It was a second or two before he was able to speak.

"These cords are killing me. Tell that friend of yours to loosen them."

"Loosen them? Why, certainly. Why not? My Skittles, loosen the cords which give Mr. Paxton so much annoyance—at once."

Skittles looked at the Baron with doubtful eyes.

"Do you mean it, Baron?"

The Baron—as the German-American was designated by Skittles—burst, without the slightest warning, into a frenzy of rage, which, although it was suggested rather than expressed, seemed to wither Skittles, root and branch, as if it had been a stroke of lightning.

"Mean it?—you idiot! How dare you ask if I mean it? Do as I say!"

Skittles lost no time in doing his best to appease the other's anger.

"You needn't be nasty, Baron. I never meant no harm. You don't always mean just exactly what you says—and that's the truth, Baron."

"Never you mind what I mean at other times—this time I mean what I say. Untie the ropes which fasten Mr. Paxton to the floor—the ropes about his hands and his feet, they are nothing, they will do very well where they are. A change of position will do him good—eh? Lift him up on to his feet, and stand him in the corner against the wall."

Skittles did as he was bid—at any rate, to the extent of unfastening the cords, which, as it were, nailed Paxton to the ground. The relief was so sudden, and, at the same time, so violent, that before he knew it, he had fainted. Fortunately, his senses did not forsake him long. He returned to consciousness just in time to hear the Baron—

"My Skittles, you get a pail of boiling water, so hot it will bring the skin right off him. It's the finest thing in the world to bring a man out of a faint—you try it, quick, you will see."

Paxton interposed, feebly—just in time to prevent the drastic prescription being given actual effect.

"You needn't put your friend to so much trouble. I must apologise for going off. I was never guilty of such a thing before. But if you had felt as I felt you might have fainted too."

"That is so—not a doubt of it. And yet, Mr. Paxton, a little time ago, if I had told you that just because a cord was untied you would faint, like a silly woman, you would have laughed at me. It is the same with fear. You think that nothing will make you afraid. My friends, and myself, we will show you. We will make you so afraid that, even if you escape with your life, and live another fifty years, you will carry your fear with you always—always—to the grave."

The Baron rubbed his long, thin, yellow hands together.

"Now, my Skittles, you will lift Mr. Paxton on to his feet, and you will stand him in the corner there, against the wall. He is very well again, in the best of health, and in the best of spirits, eh? Our friend"—there was a perceptible pause before the name was uttered—"Lawrence—you know Mr. Lawrence, my

Skittles, very well—is not yet ready to talk to our good friend Mr. Paxton—no, not quite, yet. So, till he is ready, we must keep Mr. Paxton well amused, is that not so, my Skittles, eh?"

Acting under the Baron's instructions, Skittles picked up Mr. Paxton as if he had been a child, and—although he staggered beneath the burden—carried him to the corner indicated by the other. When Cyril had been placed to the Baron's—if not to his own—satisfaction, the Baron produced from his hip-pocket a revolver. No toy affair such as one sees in England, but the sort of article which is found, and commonly carried, in certain of the Western states of America, and which thereabouts is called, with considerable propriety, a gun. This really deadly weapon the Baron proceeded to fondle in a fashion which suggested that, after all, he actually had in his heart a tenderness for something.

"Now, my Skittles, it is some time since I have had practice with my revolver; I am going to have a little practice now. I fear my hand may be a trifle out; it is necessary that a man in my position should always keep it in—eh? Mr. Paxton, I am going to amuse you very much indeed. I am a pretty fair shot—that is so. If you keep quite still—very, very still indeed—I do not think that I shall hit you, perhaps not. But, if you move ever so little, by just that little you will be hit. It will not be my fault, it will be yours, you see. I am going to singe the lobe of your left ear. Ready! Fire!"

The Baron fired.

Although released from actual bondage to the floor, Mr. Paxton was still, to all intents and purposes, completely helpless. His hands remained pinioned. Cords were wound round his legs so many times, and were drawn so tightly, that the circulation was impeded, and without support he was incapable of standing up straight on his own feet. He had no option but to confront the ingenious Baron, and to suffer him to play what tricks with him he pleased. Whatever he felt he suffered no signs of unwillingness to escape him. He looked his tormentor in the face as unflinchingly as if the weapon which he held had been a popgun. Scarcely had the shot been fired than, in one sense, if not in another, he gave the "shootist" as good as he had sent.

"You appear to be a braggart as well as a bully. You can't shoot a bit. That landed a good half-inch wide of my left ear."

"Did I not say I fear my hand is a little out? Now it is your right ear which I will make to tingle. Ready! Fire!"

Again the Baron fired.

So far as one was able to perceive, his victim did not move by so much as a hair's breadth, yet there was a splash of blood upon his cheek.

"Now I will try to put a bullet into the wall quite close to the right side of your throat. Ready! Fire!"

CHAPTER XV

PUT TO THE QUESTION

The noise of the report had not yet died away, and the cloud of smoke got wholly clear of the muzzle of the Baron's revolver, when the door of the room was thrown open to admit some one, who in low, clear, even, authoritative tones, asked a question—

"Who's making this noise?"

Whether the Baron's aim had this time been truer there was, as yet, no evidence to show. Cyril had, at any rate, escaped uninjured. At the sound of the voice, which, although it had been heard by him so seldom, had already become too familiar, he glanced round towards the questioner. It was Lawrence. He stood just inside the door, looking from the Baron to the involuntary target of that gentleman's little pleasantries. Close behind him were two men, whom Paxton immediately recognised as old acquaintances; the one was the individual who had taken a bed for the night at Makell's Hotel, who had shown such a pertinacious interest in his affairs, and whom he had afterwards suspected of an attempt to effect an entrance through his bedroom door; the second was the person who, the next morning, had followed him to the Central Station, and of whose too eager attentions he had rid himself by summoning a constable.

In the looks which Lawrence directed towards the Baron there seemed to be something both of reproach and of contempt.

"Pray, what is the meaning of this?"

The Baron made a movement in the air with one hand, then pointed with it to the revolver which he held in the other.

"My friend, it is only a little practice which I have—that is all! It is necessary that I keep my hand well in—not so—eh?"

Lawrence's voice as he replied was alive with quiet scorn.

"I would suggest that you should choose a more appropriate occasion on which to indulge yourself in what you call a little practice. Did it not occur to you, to speak of nothing else, that it might be as well to make as little, instead of as much, noise as you conveniently could?" He went and stood in front of Mr. Paxton. "I am sorry, sir, that we should meet again under such disagreeable conditions; but, as you are aware, the responsibility for what has occurred cannot, justly, be laid either on my friends or on myself."

Paxton's reply was curt. The abrupt, staccato, contemptuous tone in which he spoke was in striking contrast to Lawrence's mellifluous murmurings.

"I am aware of nothing of the sort."

Lawrence moved his head with a slight gesture of easy courtesy, which might, or might not, have been significative of his acquiescence in the other's point-blank contradiction.

"What is that upon your face—blood?"

"That is proof positive of your bungling friend's bad markmanship. He would, probably, have presented me with a few further proofs of his incapacity had you postponed your arrival for a few minutes longer."

Lawrence repeated his former courteous inclination.

"My friend is a man of an unusual humour. Apt, occasionally, like the rest of us, to rate his capacities beyond their strict deserts." He turned to the two men who had come with him into the room. "Untie Mr. Paxton's legs." Then back again to Cyril. "I regret, sir, that it is impossible for me, at the moment, to extend the same freedom to your arms and hands. But it is my sincerest trust that, in a very few minutes, we may understand each other so completely as to place it in my power to restore you, without unnecessary delay, to that position in society from which you have been withdrawn."

Although Paxton was silent outwardly, his looks were eloquent of the feelings with which he regarded the other's well-turned phrases. When his legs had been freed, the two newcomers, standing on either side of him as if they had been policemen, urged him forward, until he stood in front of the heavy table which occupied the centre of the room. On the other side of the table Lawrence had already seated himself on the only chair which the place contained. The Baron, still holding his revolver, had perched himself on a corner of the table itself. Lawrence, leaning a little forward on his chair, with one arm resting on the table, never lost his bearing of apparent impartiality, and, while he spoke with an air of quiet decision, never showed signs of a ruffled temper.

"I have already apologised to you, sir, for the discomforts which you may have endured; but, as you are aware, those discomforts you have brought upon yourself."

Paxton's lips curled, but he held his peace.

"My friends and I are in the position of men who make war upon society. As is the case in all wars, occasions arise on which exceptional measures have to be taken which, though unpleasant for all the parties chiefly concerned, are inevitable. You are an example of such an occasion."

Cyril's reply was sufficiently scornful.

"You don't suppose that your wind-bag phrases hoodwink me. You're a scoundrel; and, in consort with other scoundrels, you have taken advantage of a gentleman. I prefer to put the matter into plain English."

To this little outburst Lawrence paid no attention. For all the notice he seemed to take of them the contemptuous words might have remained unuttered.

"It is within your knowledge that, in pursuit of my profession, I appropriated the Duchess of Datchet's diamonds. I do not wish to impute to you, Mr. Paxton, acts of which you may have not been guilty; therefore I say that I think it possible it was by accident you acquired that piece of information. It is in the same spirit of leniency that I add that, at the refreshment-rooms at the Central Station, it was by mistake that you took my Gladstone bag in exchange for your own. I presume that at this time of day you do not propose to deny that such an exchange was effected. In that Gladstone bag of mine, which you took away with you by mistake instead of your own, as you know, were the Datchet diamonds. What I have now to ask you to do—and I desire, I assure you, Mr. Paxton, to ask you with all possible courtesy—is to return those diamonds at once to me, their rightful owner."

"By what process of reasoning do you make out that you are the rightful owner of the Datchet diamonds?"

"By right of conquest."

"Right of conquest! Then, following your own line of reasoning, even taking it for granted that all you have chosen to say of me is correct, I in my turn have become their rightful owner."

"Precisely. But the crux of the position is this. If the duchess could get me into her power she would stick at nothing to extort from me the restitution of the stones. In the same way, now that I have you in my power, I intend to stick at nothing which will induce their restoration from you."

"The difference between you and myself is, shortly, this—you are a thief, and I am an honest man."

"Pray, Mr. Paxton, what is your standard of honesty? If you were indeed the kind of honest man that you would appear to wish us to believe you are, you would at once have handed the stones to the police, or even have restored them to the duchess."

"How do you know that I have not?"

"I will tell you how I know. If you had been so honest there would not be in existence now a warrant to arrest you on the charge of stealing them. Things being as they are, it happens that there is."

"It's an impudent lie!"

"Possibly you may believe it to be an impudent lie; still, it is the truth. A warrant for your arrest has been granted to-day to your friend Ireland, of Scotland Yard, on his sworn information. I merely mention this as evidence that you have not handed the stones to the police, that you have not returned them to the duchess, but that you have retained them in your possession with a view of using them for purposes of your own, and that, therefore, your standard of morality is about on a level with ours."

"What you say is, from first to last, a tissue of lies. You hound! You know that! Although it is a case of five to one, my hands are tied, and so it's safe to use what words you please."

Lawrence, coming closer to the table, leaned both his elbows on the board, and crossed his arms in front of him.

"It seems, Mr. Paxton, as if you, a man of whose existence I was unaware until the other day, have set yourself to disappoint me in two of the biggest bids I have ever made for fortune and for happiness. I am a thief. It has never been made sufficiently plain to me that the difference between theft and speculation is such a vital one as to clearly establish the superiority of the one over the other. But even a thief is human—sometimes very human. I own I am. And it chances that, for some days now, I had begun to dream dreams of a most amusing kind—dreams of love—yes, and dreams of marriage. I chanced to meet a certain lady—I do not think, Mr. Paxton, that I need name any names?"

"It is a matter of indifference to me whether you do so or not."

"Thank you, very much. With this certain lady I found myself in love. I dreamt dreams of her—from which dreams I have recently arisen. A new something came into my life. I even ventured, in my new-learned presumption, to ask her would she marry me. Then for the first time I learned that what I asked for already had been given, that what I so longed for already was your own. It is strange how much one suffers from so small a thing. You'd not believe it. In our first fall, then, it seems that you have thrown me.

"Then there is this business of the Datchet jewels. A man of your experience cannot suppose that an affair of this magnitude can be arranged and finished in a moment. It needs time, and careful planning, and other things to boot. I speak as one who knows. Suppose you planned some big haul upon the Stock Exchange, collected your resources, awaited the propitious second, and, when it came, brought off your coup. If in that triumphant moment some perfect stranger were to carry off, from underneath your very nose, the spoils for which you had risked so much, and which you regarded, and rightly regarded, as your own, what would your feelings be towards such an one? Would you not feel, at least, that you would like to have his blood? If you have sufficient imagination to enable you to place yourself in such a situation, you will then be able to dimly realise what, at the present moment, our feelings are towards you."

Paxton's voice, when he spoke, was, if possible, more contemptuous than ever.

"I care nothing for your feelings."

"Precisely; and, by imparting to us that information, you make our task much easier. We, like others, can fight for our own hands—and we intend to. You see, Mr. Paxton, that, although I did the actual conveying of the diamonds, and therefore the major share of the spoil is mine, there were others concerned in the affair as well as myself, and they naturally regard themselves as being entitled to a share of the profits. You have, consequently, others to deal with as well as myself, for we, to be plain, are many. And our desire is that you should understand precisely what it is we wish to do. The first thing which we wish you to do is to tell us where, at the present moment, the diamonds are?"

"Then I won't, even supposing that I know!"

Lawrence went on without seeming to pay any heed to Cyril's unqualified refusal—

"The second thing which we wish you to do—supposing you to have placed the diamonds where it will be difficult for us to reach them—is to give us an authority which will be sufficient to enable us to demand, as your agents, if you choose, that the diamonds be handed to us without unnecessary delay."

"I will do nothing of the kind."

Again Lawrence seemed to allow the refusal to go unheeded.

"And we would like you to understand that, so soon as the diamonds are restored to us, you will be free to go, and to do, and say exactly what you please, but that you will continue to be our prisoner till they are."

"If my freedom is dependent on my fulfilling the conditions which you would seek to impose, I shall continue to be what you call your prisoner until I die; but, as it happens, my freedom is contingent on nothing of the sort, as you will find."

"We would desire, also, Mr. Paxton, that you should be under no delusion. It is far from being our intention that what, as you put it, we call your imprisonment should be a period of pleasant probation; on the contrary, we intend to make it as uncomfortable as we can—which, believe me, is saying not a little."

"That, while I am at your mercy, you will behave in a cowardly and brutal fashion I have no doubt whatever."

"More. We have no greater desire than you have yourself that you should continue to be, what we call, our prisoner. With a view, therefore, to shortening the duration of your imprisonment we shall leave no stone unturned—even if we have to resort to all the tortures of the Spanish Inquisition—to extort from you the things which we require."

Paxton laughed—shortly, dryly, scornfully.

"I don't know if your intention is to be impressive; if it is, I give you my word that you don't impress me a little bit. Your attempts to wrap up your rascality in fine-sounding phrases strike me as being typical of the sort of man you are."

"Mr. Paxton, before we come to actual business, let me advise you—and, believe me, in this case my advice is quite unprejudiced—not to treat us to any more of this kind of talk! Can't you realise that it is not for counters we are playing? That men of our sort, in our position, are not likely to stick at trifles? That it is a case of head you lose, tails we win—for, while it is obviously a fact that we have nothing we can lose, it is equally certainly a fact that there is nothing you can gain? So learn wisdom; be wise in time; endeavour to be what I would venture to call conformable. Be so good as to give me your close attention. I should be extremely obliged, Mr. Paxton, if you would give me an answer to the question which I am about to put to you. Where, at the present moment, are the Datchet diamonds?"

"I would not tell you even if I knew."

"You do know. On that point there can be no room for doubt. We mean to know, too, before we've done with you. Is that your final answer?"

"It is."

"Think again."

"Why should I think?"

"For many reasons. I will give still another chance; I will repeat my question. Before you commit yourself to a reply, do consider. Tell me where, at the present moment, are the Datchet diamonds?"

"That I will never tell you."

Mr. Lawrence made a movement with his hands which denoted disapproval.

"Since you appear to be impervious to one sort of reasoning, perhaps you may be more amenable to another kind. We will do our best to make you." Mr. Lawrence turned to the man who had been addressed as Skittles. "Be so good as to put a branding-iron into the fire, the one on which there is the word 'thief.'"

CHAPTER XVI

A MODERN INSTANCE OF AN ANCIENT PRACTICE

Skittles, when he had, apparently with an effort, mastered the nature of Mr. Lawrence's instructions, grinned from ear to ear.

He went to where a number of iron rods with broad heads were heaped together on a shelf. They were branding-irons. Selecting one of these, he thrust it into the heart of the fire which glowed on the blacksmith's furnace. He heaped fuel on to the fire. After a movement or two of the bellows it became a roaring blaze.

Lawrence turned to Mr. Paxton—

"Still once more—are you disposed to tell us where the Datchet diamonds are?"

"No."

Lawrence smiled. He addressed himself to the two men who held Paxton's arms.

"Hold him tight. Now, Skittles, bring that iron of yours. Burn a hole under Mr. Paxton's right shoulder-blade, through his clothing."

Skittles again moved the iron from the fire. It had become nearly white. He regarded it for a moment with a critical eye. Then, advancing with it held at arm's length in front of him, he took up his position at Mr. Paxton's back.

"Don't let him go. Now!"

Skittles thrust the flaming iron towards Paxton's shoulder-blade.

There was a smell of burning cloth. For a second Paxton stood like a statue; then, leaping right off his feet, he gave first a forward and then a backward bound, displaying as he did so so much vigour that, although his guardians retained their hold, Skittles, apparently, was taken unawares. Possibly, with an artist's pride in good workmanship, he had been so much engrossed by the anxiety to carry out the commission with which he had been entrusted thoroughly well, that he was unprepared for interruptions. However that may have been, when Paxton moved his grip on the iron seemed to suddenly loosen, so that, losing for the moment complete control of it, it fell down between Paxton's arms, the red-hot brand at the further end resting on his pinioned wrists. A cry as of a wounded animal, which he was totally unable to repress, came from his lips—a cry half of rage, half of agony. But the red-hot iron, while inflicting on him frightful pain, had at least done him one good service; if it had burned his flesh, it had also burned the cords which bound his wrists together. Exerting, in his passion and his agony, the strength of half a dozen men, he severed the scorched strands of rope as if they had been straws, and, hurling from him the two fellows who held his arms—who had expected nothing so little as to find his arms unbound—he stood before them, so far as his limbs were concerned, free.

Once lost, he was not to be easily regained. He was quicker in his movements than Skittles had ever been, and the latter's quickest days were long since done. Dropping on to one knee, plunging forward under Skittles' guard, he butted that gentleman with his head full in the stomach, and had snatched the iron by its handle from his astonished hands before he had fully realised what was happening. Springing with the rapidity of a jack-in-the-box, to his feet again, he brought the dreadful weapon down heavily on Skittles' head. With a groan of agony, that gentleman dropped like a log on to the floor.

Armed with the heated iron—a kind of article with which no one would care to come into close contact—Paxton turned and faced the others, who as yet did not seem fully alive to what had taken place.

"Now, you brutes! I may be bested in the end, but I'll be even with one or two of you before I am!"

Lawrence stood up.

"Will you? That still remains to be seen. Shoot him, Baron!"

The Baron fired. Either his marksmanship, or his nerve, or his something, was at fault, for he missed. Before he could fire again Paxton's weapon had crashed through his grotesquely tall high hat, and apparently through his skull as well, for he too went headlong to the floor. Quick as lightning as he fell Cyril took his revolver from his nerveless grasp. Lawrence and his two colleagues were—a little late in the day, perhaps—making for him. But when they saw how he was doubly armed and his determined front they paused—and therein showed discretion.

The tables had turned. The fortune of war had gone over to what hitherto had been distinctly the losing side. So at least Paxton appeared to think.

"Now, the question is, what shall I do with you? Shall I shoot all three of you—or shall I brain one of you with this pretty little play-thing, which I have literally snatched from the burning?"

If one could draw deductions from the manner in which he bore himself, Lawrence never for an instant lost his presence of mind. When he spoke it was in the easy, quiet tones which he had used throughout.

"You move too fast, forgetting two things—one, that you are caught here like a rat in a trap, so that, unless we choose to let you, you cannot get out of this place alive; the other, that I have only to summon assistance to overwhelm you with the mere force of numbers."

"Then why don't you summon assistance, if you are so sure that it will come at your bidding?"

"I intend to summon assistance when I choose."

"I give you warning that, if you move so much as a muscle in an attempt to attract the attention of any other of your associates who may be about the place, I will shoot you!"

For answer Lawrence smiled. Suddenly, lifting his hand, he put two fingers to his lips and blew a loud, shrill, peculiar whistle. Simultaneously Paxton raised the revolver, and, pointing it straight at the other's head, he pulled the trigger.

And that was all. No result ensued. There was the sound of a click—and nothing more. His face darkened. A second time he pulled the trigger; again without result. Mr. Lawrence's smile became more pronounced. His tone was one of gentle badinage.

"I thought so. You see, you will move too quickly. It is a six-chambered revolver. I was aware that my highly esteemed friend had discharged two barrels earlier in the evening, and had not reloaded. I knew that he had taken two, if not three, little pops at you, and had had another little pop just now. If, therefore, he had not recharged in my absence the barrels I had seen him empty, and had taken, before I interrupted him, three little pops at you, the revolver must be empty. I thought the risk worth taking, and I took it."

While Cyril seemed to hesitate as to what to do next, Lawrence, raising his fingers to his lips, blew another cat-call.

While the shrill discord still travelled through the air, Paxton sprang towards him. Stepping back, the whistler, picking up the wooden chair on which he had been sitting, dashed it in his assailant's face. And at the same moment the two men who had hitherto remained passive spectators of what had been, practically, an impromptu if abortive duel, closed in on Paxton from either side.

He struck at one with his clubbed revolver. The other, getting his arm about his throat, dragged him backwards on to the floor. He was down, however, only for a second. Slipping from the fellow's grasp like an eel, he was up again in time to meet the renewed attack from the man whom he had already struck with his revolver. He struck at him again; but still the man was not disabled.

Meanwhile, his more prudent companion, conducting his operations from the rear, again got his arms about Paxton. The three went in a heap together on the floor.

Just then the door was opened and some one entered on the scene. Paxton did not stop to see who it was. Exercising what seemed to be a giant's strength, he succeeded in again freeing himself from the grasp of his two opponents. Leaping to his feet, he made a mad dash at Lawrence. That gentleman, springing nimbly aside, eluded the threatening blow from the clubbed revolver, delivered neatly enough a blow with his clenched fist full in Mr. Paxton's face. The blow was a telling one. Mr. Paxton staggered; then, just as he seemed about to fall, recovered himself, and struck again at Mr. Lawrence. This time the blow went home. The butt of the revolver came down upon the other's head with a sickening thud. The stricken man flung up his arms, and, without a sound, collapsed in an invertebrate heap.

The whole place became filled with confusion and shouts.

With what seemed to be a sudden inspiration, swinging right round, with the branding-iron, which he had managed to retain in his possession, Paxton struck at the hanging lamp, which was suspended from the ceiling. In a moment the atmosphere began to be choked by the suffocating fumes of burning oil. A sheet of fire was running across the floor. Heedless of all else, Paxton rushed towards the door.

Such was the confusion occasioned by the disappearance of the lamp, and by the appearance of the flames, that his frantic flight seemed for the moment to be unnoticed. He tore through the door, up a narrow flight of steps rising between two walls, which he found in front of him, only, however, to find an individual awaiting his arrival at the top. This individual was evidently one who deemed that there are cases in which discretion is the better part of valour, and that the present case was one of them. When Paxton appeared, instead of trying to arrest his progress, he moved hastily aside, evincing, indeed, a conspicuous unwillingness to offer him any impediment in his wild career. Paxton passed him. There was a door in front of him. In his mad haste, throwing it open, he went through it. In an instant it was banged behind him; he heard the sound of a bolt being shot home into its socket, and of a voice exclaiming with a chuckle—on the other side of the door!—

"Couldn't have done it better if I'd tried, I couldn't! Locked hisself in—straight he has!"

Too late Paxton learned that, to all intents and purposes, that was exactly what he had done.

The place in which he found himself was pitchy dark. He had supposed that it might be a passage leading to a door beyond. It proved to be nothing of the kind. It seemed, instead, to be some sort of cupboard— probably a pantry—for he could feel that there were shelves on either side of him, and that on the shelves were what seemed to be victuals. Though narrow, by stretching out his arms he could feel the wall with either hand; it extended, longitudinally, to some considerable distance—possibly to twenty feet. At the further end there was a window. It was at an inconvenient height from the floor, and directly under it was a shelf. On this shelf, so far as he was able to judge, was an indiscriminate collection of pieces of crockery. The shelf, however, was a broad one, and, disregarding the various impedimenta with which it seemed to be covered, by clambering on to it he was brought within easy reach of the window. It was a small one, and had two sashes. Had the sashes not been there, there might have been sufficient space to enable him to thrust his body through the frame. They were of the ordinary kind, moving up and down, and, in consequence, when they were open to their widest extent, only half the window space was available either for ingress or for egress.

He did throw up the lower sash as far as it would go, only to discover that it scarcely gave him room enough to put the whole of his head outside. Taking firm hold of the framework, he tested its solidity; it appeared to be substantially constructed of some kind of heavy wood. Though he exerted considerable force, it could hardly be induced to rattle. To remove it, even if it was removable, would be a work of time and of labour. Time he had not at his command. Although he was fastened in, his assailants were not fastened out. At any moment they might enter; his struggles—against such odds!—would have to be recommenced all over again.

He was conscious that the best of his strength was spent. He was stiff and sore, weary and bewildered. Nor had he escaped uninjured. He was covered with bruises—bruises which ached. Where the red-hot branding-iron, slipping from Mr. Skittles' grasp, had struck against his wrists, the flesh felt as if it had been burnt to the bone; it occasioned him exquisite pain. No, in his present plight, recapture would be easy. After the recent transactions, in which he had played so prominent a figure, recapture would mean nameless tortures, if not death outright. His only hope lay in flight, or—the thought came to him as he was endeavouring to marshal his faculties in sufficient order to enable him to take an impartial view of his position—in summoning help.

Summoning help? Yes! why not? The thing was feasible. Here was the open window. He could call through it. His cries might be heard, and if he could only make his shouts heard by some one without the alarm would be raised, and he would soon be rescued from this den of thieves.

Thrusting his head out as far as possible, he shouted, with might and with main—"Help! Murder! Help!"

He listened. He seemed to hear the faint echo of his own words travelling mockingly, mournfully, through the silent air. Naught else was audible. All else was still as the grave.

Nor did the prospect of his being able to make himself heard seem promising.

He had no notion whereabouts the house in which he was so unwilling a guest was situated. In front of him he could see nothing but open space. There was neither moon nor stars, nor was the atmosphere particularly clear; yet, as his eyes grew more accustomed to the darkness, it seemed to him that he could see for miles, and that there was nothing to be seen. There was not a light in sight; no glare of lights upon the distant sky; the shadow neither of a house nor of a tree. No murmur of voices; no hum of far-off traffic; not even the unceasing turmoil of the restless sea.

Since, so far as he was able to perceive, the place seemed to be given up to such utter and entire solitude, it struck him with unpleasant force that it might be located in the very heart of the open Downs. In that case it was quite upon the cards that there was not another human habitation within miles. At night—even yet!—few places are more deserted than the Brighton Downs. All sorts of deeds without a name, so far as human witnesses are concerned, can be wrought thereon with complete impunity.

If the house was really built upon the Downs, his chances of making himself heard were remote indeed. Still, in his desperate position, he was not disposed to give up hope without making at least another trial. Once more he shouted "Help! Murder! Help!"

Again he listened. And this time, from what evidently was a considerable distance, there was borne through the night what seemed to be an answering call—"Hollo!"

Seldom was so slight a sound so grateful to a listener's ears!

With renewed ardour he repeated his shouts, with, if possible, even greater vigour than before: "Quick! Help! Murder! Help!"

Again, from afar, there seemed to come the faint response—"Hollo!"

And at the same instant he became conscious of voices speaking together outside the door of the cul-de-sac in which, foolishly enough, he had allowed himself to be made, for a second time, a prisoner.

CHAPTER XVII

THE MOST DANGEROUS FOR OF ALL

Mr. Paxton withdrew his face from the window. He turned towards the door, his ears wide open. The speakers were talking so loudly that he could hear distinctly, without moving from his post of vantage on the shelf, every word which was uttered. They seemed to be in a state of great excitement.

The first voice he heard belonged evidently to the quick-witted individual who had fastened him in the trap which he himself had entered.

"There he is—inside there he is—ran in of his own accord he did, so I shut the door, and I slipped the bolt before he knowed where he was. The winder's only a little 'un—if he gets hisself out, you can call me names."

The second voice was one which Mr. Paxton did not remember to have previously noticed.

"Blast him!—what do I care where he is? He ain't no affair of mine! There's the Toff, and a crowd of 'em down there—you come and lend a hand!"

"Not me! I ain't a-taking any! I ain't going to get myself choked, not for no Toff, nor yet for any one else. I feel more like cutting my lucky—only I don't know my way across these — hills."

"You ain't got no more pluck than a chicken. Go and put the 'orse in! Me and them other two chaps will bring 'em up. We shall have to put the whole lot aboard, and make tracks as fast as the old mare will canter."

A third voice became audible—a curiously husky one, as if its owner was in difficulties with his throat.

"Here's the Toff—he seems to be a case. I ain't a-going down no more. It's no good a-trying to put it out—you might as well try to put out 'ell fire!"

Then a fourth voice—even huskier than the other.

"Catch 'old! If some one don't catch 'old of the Baron I shall drop 'im. My God! this is a pretty sort of go!"

There was a pause, then the voice of the first speaker again.

"He do look bad, the Baron do—worse nor the Toff, and he don't seem too skittish!"

"Strikes me he ain't far off from a coffin and a six-foot 'ole. You wouldn't look lively if you'd had what he 'as. That there — brained 'im, and now he's been burned alive. I tell you what it is, we shall have to look slippy if we want to get ourselves well out of this. Them others will have to scorch—it's no good trying to get 'em out—no mortal creature could live down there—it'll only be a bit sooner, anyhow. The whole — place is like a — tinder-box. It'll all be afire in less than no time, and it'll make a bonfire as'll be seen over all the countryside; and if we was seen a-making tracks away from it, there might be questions asked, and we mightn't find that pretty!"

"Where's the — as done it all?"

"In there—that's where he is!"

"In there? Sure? My—! wouldn't I like to strip his skin from off his — carcase!"

"He'll have his skin stripped off from him without your doing nothing, don't you be afraid—and made crackling of! He'll never get outside of that—he'll soon be warm enough—burnt to a cinder, that's what he'll be!"

Suddenly there was a tumult of exclamations and of execrations, sound of the opening of a door, and of a general stampede. Then silence.

And Mr. Paxton realised to the full what had happened. For into the place of his imprisonment there penetrated, all at once, the fumes of smoke—fumes which had an unpleasantly irritating effect upon the tonsils of his throat.

The house was on fire! The hanging-lamp which he had sent crashing to the floor had done its work—had, indeed, plainly, done more than he intended. Nothing so difficult to extinguish as the flames of burning oil. Nothing which gets faster, fiercer, more rapidly increasing hold—nothing which, in an incredibly short space of time, causes more widespread devastation.

The house was on fire! and he was caged there like a rat in a trap! The smoke already reached him—already the smell of the fire was in his nostrils. And those curs, those cowards, those nameless brutes, thinking only of their wretched selves, had left their comrades in that flaming, fiery furnace, to perish by the most hideous of deaths, and had left him, also, there to burn.

In a sudden paroxysm of rage, leaping off the shelf, he rushed to the opposite end of what, it seemed, bade fair to be his crematorium, and flung himself with all his weight and force against the door. It never yielded—he might as well have flung himself against the wall. He shouted through it, like a madman—

"Open the door! Open the door, you devils!"

In his frenzy a stream of oaths came flooding from his lips. In such situations even clean-mouthed men can swear. There are not many of us who, brought suddenly, under such circumstances, face to face with the hereafter, can calm our minds and keep watch and ward over our tongues. Mr. Paxton, certainly, was not such an one. He was, rather, as one who was consumed with fury.

What was that? He listened. It was the sound of wheels and of a horse's hoofs. Those scoundrels were off—fleeing for their lives. And he was there—alone! And in the dreadful furnace, at the bottom of that narrow flight of steps, the miserable creatures with whom he had had such a short and sharp reckoning were being burned.

In his narrow chamber the presence of smoke was becoming more conspicuous. He could hear the crackling of fire. It might have been imagination, but it seemed to him that already the temperature was increasing. What was he to do? He recollected the window—clambered back upon the shelf, and thrust his face out into the open air. How sweet it was! and fresh, and cool! Once more he listened. He could hear, plainly enough, the noise of wheels rolling rapidly away, but nothing more. With the full force of his lungs he repeated his previous cry, with a slight variation—

"Help! Fire! Help!"

But this time there came no answering "Hollo!" There was no reply. Again he shouted, and again and again, straining his throat and his lungs to bursting-point, screaming himself hoarse, but there was none that answered. It seemed that this was a case in which, if he could not help himself, he, in very deed and in very truth, was helpless.

He set himself to remove the sashes from their places, feeling that if he only could, small even then though the space would be, he might, at such a pinch as this, be able to squeeze his body through. But the thing was easier essayed than done. The sashes were small, strongly constructed, and solidly set in firmly fashioned grooves. He attacked them with his hands; he hammered them with the Baron's revolver and the branding-iron, but they remained precisely where they were. He had a suspicion that they were looser, and that in time, say in an hour or so, they might be freed. But he had not an hour to spare. He had not many minutes, for while he still wrestled with their obstinacy there came from behind him a strange, portentous roar. His prison became dimly, fitfully illuminated with a dreadful light—so that he could see.

What he could see through the cracks in the bolted door were tongues of fire, roaring in the room beyond—roaring as the waves roar over the stones, or as the sound of a high wind through the tops of trees. The suddenness of the noise, disturbing so unexpectedly the previous stillness, confused him. He remained on the shelf, looking round. Then, oblivious for the moment of the danger which so swiftly was coming nearer, he was filled with admiration. What a beautiful ruddy light it was, which was making the adjacent chamber to gleam like glowing gold! How every instant it was becoming ruddier and ruddier, until, with fairylike rapidity, it became a glorious blaze of colour! The whole place was transfigured and transformed. It was radiant with the splendours of the Fairy Queen's Palace of a Million Marvels.

The crackling noise which fire makes when its hungry tongues lick woodwork brought him back to a sense of stern reality. He became conscious of the strong breeze which was blowing through the open window. It was coming from the house, and was bearing with it a rush as of heated breath. Already it seemed to scorch his cheeks—momentarily it seemed to scorch them more and more. The air, as he drew it into his lungs, was curiously dry. He had to draw two breaths where before he had drawn one. It parched his throat. What would he not have given to have been able to glue his lips to cool, fresh water! As in a vision he pictured himself laving his face, splashing in the crystal waters of a running stream, with the trees in leaf above his head.

Escape was hopeless. Neither on the one side nor on the other could salvation be attained. Other men, he told himself, with a sardonic twitching of the corners of his lips, had been burnt alive before to-day—then why not he? He, at any rate, could play the man. To attempt to strive against the inevitable was puerile. Better, if one must die, "facing fearful odds," to die with one's arms folded, and with one's pulse marking time at its normal pace. What must be, might be; what cared he?

Confound the smoke! It came in thicker and thicker wreaths through the interstices in the panels of the door. It was impossible to continue facing it; it made him cough, and the more he coughed the more he had to. It got into his mouth and up his nose; it made his eyes tingle. To cough and cough until, like a ramshackle cart, one shook oneself to pieces, was not the part of dignity.

He turned his back to the door. He thrust his face again through the window. With his lips wide open he gulped in the air with a sense of rapture which amounted to positive pain. What a feeling of life and of freedom there seemed to be under the stars and the far-reaching sky! What a spirit of solitude was abroad on the hills, in the darkness of the night! What a lonely death this was which he was about to die! No one there but God and the fire to see if he died like a man!

He tried to collect his thoughts. As he did so, there was borne to him, on a sudden overwhelming flood of recollection, the woman whom he loved. He seemed to see her there in front of him—her very face. What was she doing now? What would she do if she had an inkling of his plight? What, when she knew that he had gone? If he had only had time to hand over to her all the fruits of that rise in the shares of the Trumpit Gold Mine!

How hot it was! And the smoke—how suffocating! How the fire roared behind him! The bolted door had been stout enough to keep him captive, but against the fury of the flames it would be as nothing. Any moment they might be through. And then?

He had an inspiration. He began to feel in his pockets. Those rogues had stripped them, only leaving, so far as in his haste he could judge, two worthless trifles, which probably had been overlooked because of their triviality. In one pocket was the back of an old letter, in another a scrap of pencil. They were sufficient to serve his purpose. Spreading the half-sheet of notepaper out on the shelf in front of him, he wrote, as well as he could for the blinding, stifling smoke, with the piece of pencil—

"I give and bequeath all that I have in the world to my dear love, Daisy Strong, who would have been my wife. God bless her!—CYRIL PAXTON."

CHAPTER XVIII

THE LAST OF THE DATCHET DIAMONDS

They found him, with the half-sheet of notepaper all crushed in his hand.

At the police station, acting on the hints dropped by Mr. Cooper, Mr. Ireland had enlisted the aid of a dozen constables. He had chartered a large waggonette, and with Mr. Cooper and a sergeant beside him on the box-seat had started off for an evening drive across the Downs. Miss Strong had, perforce, to content herself with a seat with Miss Wentworth and Mr. Franklyn in a fly behind.

The weather had cleared. By the time they reached the open country the stars were shining, and when they found themselves following the winding road among the hills it was as fine a night as one could wish. Suddenly the occupants of the fly became conscious that the waggonette in front had stopped. A constable, hurrying back, checked the flyman. Miss Strong leant over the side of the vehicle to address him.

"What is the matter?"

"We don't know yet, miss. Only there's something coming along the road, and we want to see what they look like. They seem to be in a bit of a hurry."

As the man said, whoever it was who was approaching did seem to be in a "bit of a hurry." Evidently the horse in the advancing vehicle was being urged to a breakneck gallop. Where the waggonette had stopped the ground rose abruptly on either side. The road turned sharply just in front. The constables, alighting, formed in double line across it. Suddenly the people who were hastening Brightonwards found themselves quite unexpectedly surrounded by the officers of the law. There was the liveliest five minutes Miss Strong had ever known. At the end of it the police found themselves in possession of three prisoners, who had fought as well as, under the circumstances, they knew how, and also of a fly with two men lying apparently dead inside it.

When Miss Strong learnt this, she came hurrying up.

"Is Cyril there?"

Mr. Ireland shook his head.

"You are telling me the truth?"

"If you doubt it, Miss Strong, you may look for yourself."

Just then a constable who, for purposes of observation, had climbed the sloping ground on one side of the road, gave a great shout.

"Fire! There's a house on fire on the hills!"

Mr. Cooper, who, while his former friends were being captured, had, much against his will, been handcuffed to a policeman, called to Mr. Ireland.

"I reckon it's the crib. They been and set it afire, and left the bloke as they calls Paxton to burn inside of it. See if they ain't!"

It was Miss Strong who found him. Running round the burning building, she came to a little open window through which a man's hand was stretched. The window was too high above the ground to enable her to see into it. Only the hand was visible. She thought it belonged to some one who was seeking to escape.

"Who are you?" she cried.

None answered. She touched the hand, supposing its owner did not hear. As she did so a piece of crumpled paper fell out of it. She caught at it as it fluttered through the air; looked at it—there was a sufficiency of artificial light to enable her to see—saw her own name—"my dear love, Daisy Strong"— staring her in the face; perceived that it was in the writing which she knew so well.

"Cyril, Cyril!"

She snatched at the hand which had held that paper—testimony of a love which was resolute to live even beyond the grave—sprang up at the window, through which the smoke was streaming, with the flames beginning to follow after—broke into shrieks. They brought tools, and having by their aid removed the sashes, they dragged him by main force through the window, through which he himself had vainly endeavoured to escape. And slowly, enduring as he went not a little agony, he went through the Valley of the Shadow, branching out of it after all through a pass which led, not unto Death, but back again to the Plain of Life.

When, weeks after, he opened his eyes to consciousness, the first thing he saw was, leaning over him, the face of the woman he loved.

"Daisy!"

In an attenuated whisper the name came from his lips. And, forgetting herself, she fell on his breast and kissed him, and in the tumult of her joy cried as if her heart would break. While still his life was in the balance, never once had she lost her self-control, fearing that if she did she might be banished from his presence. Now that the event seemed clear, the cisterns of her heart were opened, and she wept as one distraught.

As the days went by Mr. Paxton understood not only that he was in a bedroom in Miss Wentworth's house, but also that in the adjacent apartment there was something, or some one, whose presence Miss Strong, at any rate, was desirous should be concealed from him. The thing becoming more and more conspicuous, Mr. Paxton insisted at last on having the mystery explained to him. With flashing eyes and faltering lips Miss Strong explained.

In the room adjoining that in which he lay was a policeman. He had been there all the time. He intended to remain, at least, as long as Mr. Paxton stayed. Mr. Paxton was, in fact, a prisoner—a prisoner in Miss Wentworth's house. Since it had seemed likely that he would die, the authorities had suffered him to be committed to the hands of friends, in order that, if they could, they might nurse him back to health and strength. But not for an instant had he been out of official supervision. Egress from the sick-chamber was only possible by passing through the adjoining room; in that adjoining room a policeman had been stationed night and day. Now that he was mending, at any moment rough, unfeeling hands might drag him off to gaol.

Miss Strong's manner, as she made the situation clear to Mr. Paxton, was reminiscent of the Tragic Muse. Her rage against Mr. Ireland was particularly fierce. When she spoke of him it was with clenched fists and knitted brows and eyes like flaming coals.

"He actually dares to pretend to think that you had something to do with the stealing of the Datchet diamonds."

Mr. Paxton seemed to hesitate; then took her breath away with his answer.

"He is right in thinking so; I had."

She was standing at his bedside. When he said that, she looked down at him as if she felt either that her ears must be playing her false or that he must be still delirious. Yet he seemed to speak rationally, and although pale and wan and but the shadow of his old self, he did not look as if he were insane.

"Cyril! You don't understand me. I say that he thinks that you had something to do with the stealing of the Datchet diamonds—some improper connection with the crime, I mean."

"I understand you perfectly well, my dear. I repeat, I had."

She sat down on a chair and gasped.

"You had! Goodness gracious! What?"

"After they had been stolen. The diamonds came into my possession owing to an accident."

"Cyril! Whatever did you do with them?"

"They are in my possession now."

"The Datchet diamonds! In your possession! Where?"

Her eyes, opened at their widest, were round as saucers. She was a living note of exclamation. Obviously, though he did not seem as though he were, she felt that he must be still delirious. He quickly made it plain to her, however, that he was nothing of the kind. He told her, clearly and succinctly, the whole strange history—nothing extenuating, attempting in no whit to whitewash the blackness of his own offending—precisely as it all occurred. And when his tale was at an end, instead of reproaching him by so much as a look, she kissed him, and, pillowing her lovely head upon his undeserving breast, anointed him with her tears, as if by what his criminality had cost him he had earned for himself a niche in hagiology. Later, he repeated the story to Mr. Franklyn and to Mr. Ireland. Neither of them were moved to show signs of sympathy. Plainly his friend was of opinion that, at the very least, he had played the fool; while the detective, whose moral sensibilities had perhaps been dulled by his constant contact with crime, seemed to be struck rather by his impudence than by anything else.

Mr. Paxton having voluntarily furnished Mr. Ireland with sufficient authority to enable him to gain access to the safe which he rented in that stronghold in Chancery Lane, the diamonds were found reposing securely in its fastnesses, exactly as he had described. Her Grace of Datchet's heart was gladdened by the knowledge that her priceless treasures would be returned to her in the same condition in which they left her. And the thing, being noised abroad, became a nine days' wonder.

The law is very beautiful in its tender mercies. The honest man, being sick, may die in a ditch, and no one cares. On the ailing criminal are lavished all the resources of medical science. Mr. Lawrence and his friend the Baron were far too precious in the eyes of the law to be allowed to die. It was absolutely indispensable that such unmitigated scoundrels should be kept alive. And they were. Although, had not the nicest skill been continually at their disposal, they had been dead a dozen times. Not only had Mr. Paxton broken both their skulls—well broken them too—with a breaking that required not a little mending; but, as if that were not enough, they had been nearly incinerated on top of it. However, the unremitting attention with which the law provided them, because they were such rogues, sufficed to pull them through. And at last there came a day on which they were sufficiently recovered to permit of their taking their places in the dock in order that they might be charged with their offences.

The prisoners who stood before the magistrates, charged with various degrees of complicity in the robbery of the Duchess of Datchet's diamonds, were, to begin with, six in number. First and foremost was Reginald Hargraves, alias Arthur Lawrence, alias "The Toff," alias, in all probability, twenty other names. From the beginning to the end he bore himself with perfect self-possession, never leading any one to suppose, either by look or gesture, that he took any particular amount of interest in what was going on. A second was Isaac Bergstein, alias "The Baron." His behaviour, especially when the chief and most damning testimony was being given against him, was certainly not marked by the repose which, if we are to believe the poet, is a characteristic of the caste of Vere de Vere. Cyril Paxton was a third; while the tail consisted of the three gentlemen who had fallen into the hands of the Philistines on the road to Brighton.

Before the case was opened the counsel for the prosecution intimated that he proposed to offer no evidence against the defendant, Cyril Paxton, but, with the permission of the Bench, would call him as a witness for the Crown. The Bench making no objection, Mr. Paxton stepped from the dock to the box, his whilom fellow-prisoners following him on his passage with what were very far from being looks of love.

Mr. William Cooper and Mr. Paxton were the chief witnesses for the prosecution. It was they who made the fate of the accused a certainty. Mr. Cooper, in particular, had had with them such long and such an intimate acquaintance that the light which he was enabled to cast on their proceedings was a vivid one. At the same time, beyond all sort of doubt, Mr. Paxton's evidence was the sensation of the case. Seldom has a more curious story than that which he unfolded been told, even in that place in which all the strangest stories have been told, a court of justice. He had more than one bad quarter of an hour, especially at the hands of cross-examining counsel. But, when he was finally allowed to leave the box, it was universally felt that, so far as hope of escape for the prisoners was concerned, already the case was over. Their defenders would have to work something like a miracle if Mr. Paxton's evidence was to be adequately rebutted.

That miracle was never worked. When the matter came before the judge at the assizes, his lordship's summing-up was brief and trenchant, and, without leaving their places, the jury returned a verdict of guilty against the whole of the accused. Mr. Hargraves and Mr. Bergstein—who have figured in these pages under other names—was each sent to penal servitude for twenty years, their colleagues being sentenced to various shorter periods of punishment. Mr. Hargraves—or Mr. Lawrence, whichever you please—bowed to the judge with quiet courtesy as he received his sentence. Mr. Bergstein, or the "Baron," however, looked as if he felt disposed to signify his sentiments in an altogether different fashion.

CHAPTER XIX

A WOMAN'S LOGIC

The boom in the shares of the Trumpit Gold Mine continued long enough to enable Mr. Paxton to realise his holding, if not at the top price—that had been touched while he had been fighting for his life in bed—still for a sum which was large enough to ensure his complete comfort, so far as pecuniary troubles were concerned, for the rest of his life. It was his final speculation. The ready money which he obtained he invested in consols. He lives on the interest, and protests that nothing will ever again induce him to gamble in stocks and shares. Since a lady who is largely interested in his movements has endorsed his promise, it is probable that he will keep his word.

Immediately after the trial Mr. Cyril Paxton and Miss Daisy Strong were married quietly at a certain church in Brighton; if you find their names upon its register of marriages you will know which church it was. In the first flush of his remorse and self-reproach—one should always remember that "when the devil was ill, the devil a saint would be"—Mr. Paxton declared that his conduct in connection with the Datchet diamonds had made him unworthy of an alliance with a decent woman. When he said this, urged thereto by his new-born humility and sense of shame, Miss Strong's conduct really was outrageous. She abused him for calling himself unworthy, asserted that all along she had known that, when it came to the marrying-point, he meant to jilt her; and that, since her expectations on that subject were now so fully realised, to her most desperate undoing, all that there remained for her to do was to throw herself into the sea from the end of the pier. She vowed that everything had been her fault, exclaiming that if she had never fallen away from the high estate which is woman's proper appanage, so far as to accept of the shelter of Mr. Lawrence's umbrella in that storm upon the Dyke, but suffered herself to be drowned and blown to shreds instead, nothing would have happened which had happened; and that, therefore, all the evil had been wrought by her. Though she had never thought— never for an instant—that he would, or could, have been so unforgiving! When she broke into tears, affirming that, in the face of his hardheartedness, nothing was left to her but death, he succumbed to this latest example of the beautiful simplicity of feminine logic, and admitted that he might after all be a more desirable parti than he had himself supposed.

"You have passed through the cleansing fires," she murmured, when, her reasoning having prevailed, a reconciliation had ensued. "And you have issued from them, if possible, truer metal than you went in."

Mr. Paxton felt that that indeed was very possible. He allowed the compliment to go unheeded— conscious, no doubt, that it was undeserved.

"God grant that I may never again be led into such temptation!"

That was what he said. We, on our part, may hope that his prayer may be granted.

Richard Marsh – A Short Biography

Richard Bernard Heldmann was born on 12th October 1857, in St Johns Wood, North London, to parents Joseph Heldmann and Emma Marsh.

Shortly after his birth his father became ensnared in a bankruptcy proceedings which enforced the abandonment of a career as a merchant for that of a schoolmaster at a school in Hammersmith, West London.

By his early 20's the young Heldmann, showing a talent for writing, began publishing fiction. In 1880, he began to publish works of boys' school and adventure stories for the myriad magazine publications all eager for good well-written content. The most important of these was Union Jack, one of the better quality boys' weekly magazine associated with the popular authors G. A. Henty and W.H.G. Kingston.

Heldmann was promoted to co-editor in October 1882, but his association with the publication ended suddenly in June 1883. After this, Heldmann published no further fiction under that name.

The reason at the time was not immediately apparent but in April 1884 Heldmann was sentenced to 18 months of hard labour for issuing a series of cheques, all forged, in France and Britain the year before.

In order to be well away from the scandal and damage this had caused to his reputation Heldmann adopted a pseudonym on his release from jail. Shortly thereafter the name 'Richard Marsh' began to appear in the literary periodicals. The use of his mother's maiden name seems both a release from the criminal record now associated with his given name and a lifeline to a fresh beginning.

A stroke of very good fortune arrived when his novel The Beetle was published in 1897. There had been more than a few previous publications of his works but The Beetle would turn out to be his greatest commercial success and added some much-needed gravitas to his literary reputation. The story concerns a mysterious oriental person who follows a British politician to London, and then wreaks havoc with his powers of hypnosis and shape-shifting. The Beetle has some similar aspects to certain other novels of the period, including those such as Bram Stoker's Dracula, George du Maurier's Trilby, and Sax Rohmer's many Fu Manchu novels. Like Dracula, and also the sensation novels written by Wilkie Collins and others during the 1860s, The Beetle is narrated from the various viewpoints of multiple characters to create suspense. The novel is also layered with many themes and issues of the Victorian era including women's rights, unemployment, urban poverty, radical politics, homosexuality, science, and Britain's imperial adventures, particularly in regard to Egypt and the Sudan. The Beetle sold out upon its initial print run and thereafter sold well for the next several decades. After Marsh's early death the novel's story was made into a film and adapted for the London stage, both in the 1920's.

It should also be noted that in the year of its first publication it outsold Dracula, then also in its first year of publication. In hindsight a remarkable achievement.

Marsh was a prolific writer and wrote almost 80 volumes of fiction as well as many short stories, across several genres from horror and crime to romance and humour.

However, at horror he was particularly adept. Works such as The Goddess: A Demon (1900), in which an Indian sacrificial idol comes to life with murderous resolve, and The Joss: A Reversion (1901), whose central premise is that of an Englishman who transforms himself into a hideous oriental idol are prime examples.

An important element of many of Marsh's novels is the investigation of the mystery. Several of his novels are centered on the crime and its subsequent detection. In the novel Philip Bennion's Death (1897) a bachelor is discovered dead the day after discussing Thomas De Quincey's essay on murder as a fine art, and his neighbour and friend begin efforts to solve his death. In The Datchet Diamonds (1898) a young man who has lost a fortune on the stock market mistakenly swaps bags with a diamond thief, and then find himself pursued by both the thieves and police. In A Spoiler of Men (1905), Marsh puts together crime and science-fiction; the gentleman-criminal villain renders people slaves to his will by a chemical injection.

As with many authors success with popular fiction was never quite enough. He also wanted to be regarded as a serious author. His novel A Second Coming (1900) imagines Christ's return to an early-20th century London and is his most well-handled attempt in that pursuit.

His prolific output of short stories ensured his being published in a plethora of magazines including Household Words, Cornhill Magazine, The Strand Magazine, and Belgravia, as well as in a number of short story book collections. These collections; The Seen and the Unseen (1900), Marvels and Mysteries (1900), Both Sides of the Veil (1901) and Between the Dark and the Daylight (1902) all feature an eclectic mix of humour, crime, romance and the occult.

He also published several serial short stories. Here he was able to develop characters whose adventures could be related in discrete stories across numerous editions of a magazine. An example is Mr. Pugh and Mr. Tress of Curios (1898). They are rival collectors between whom pass a series of bizarre and disturbing objects—poisoned rings, pipes which seem to come to life, a phonograph record on which a murdered woman seems to speak from the dead, and the severed hand of a 13th-century aristocrat.

During his career he sometimes came up with characters or stories ahead of their time. His character Miss Judith Lee, a young teacher of deaf pupils whose lip-reading ability involves her with mysteries that she solves by acting as a detective was very pro-active in this regard.

Richard Marsh died from heart disease in Haywards Heath in Sussex on 9th August 1915.

Several of his novels were published posthumously.

Richard Marsh – A Concise Bibliography

As Bernard Heldmann
Boxall School: A Tale of Schoolboy Life (1881)
Dorrincourt [Union Jack, April-September 1881]
Expelled: Being the Story of a Young Gentleman (1882)
Daintree (1883)

As Richard Marsh
Capturing a Convict (Strand Magazine 1893)
The Devil's Diamond (1893)
The Mahatma's Pupil (1893)
The Strange Wooing of Mary Bowler (1895)
Mrs Musgrave—and her Husband (1895)
The Mystery of Philip Bennion's Death (1897)
The Crime and the Criminal (1897)
The Duke and the Damsel (1897)
The Beetle: A Mystery (1897)
The House of Mystery (1898)
Under One Cover: Eleven Stories by S. Baring-Gould, Richard Marsh, Ernest G. Henham, Fergus Hume, Andrew Merry and A. St John Adcock (1898)
Curios: Some Strange Adventures of Two Bachelors (1898)
Tom Ossington's Ghost (1898)
The Datchet Diamonds (1898)
The Woman with One Hand and Mr Ely's Engagement (1899)
In Full Cry (1899)
Frivolities: Especially Addressed to Those Who Are Tired of Being Serious (1899)
The Purse Which Was Found

For One Night Only
Returning a Verdict
The Chancellor's Ward
A Honeymoon Trip
The Burglar's Blunder
Ninepence
A Battlefield Up-to-date
Mr. Harland's Pupils
A Burglar Alarm
A Lesson in Sculling
Outside
The Chase of the Ruby (1900)
An Aristocratic Detective (1900)
A Hero of Romance (1900)
The Seen and the Unseen (1900)
The Goddess: A Demon (1900)
Ada Vernham, Actress (1900)
A Second Coming (1900)
Marvels and Mysteries (1900)
The Long Arm of Coincidence
The Mask
An Experience
Pourquoipas
By Suggestion
A Silent Witness
To Be Used Against Him
The Words of a Little Child
How He Passed!
The Joss: A Reversion (1901)
Both Sides of the Veil (1901)
Amusement Only (1901)
The Twickenham Peerage (1902)
Between the Dark and the Daylight (1902)
The Adventures of Augustus Short: Things Which I Have Done for Others and Wish I Hadn't (1902)
A Metamorphosis (1903)
The Death Whistle (1903)
The Magnetic Girl (1903)
Miss Arnott's Marriage (1904)
Garnered (1904)
A Duel (1904)
A Spoiler of Men (1905)
The Marquis of Putney (1905)
The Confessions of a Young Lady (1905)
Under One Flag (1906)
In the Service of Love (1906)
The Garden of Mystery (1906)
A Woman Perfected (1907)
The Romance of a Maid of Honour (1907)

The Girl and the Miracle (1907)
The Surprising Husband (1908)
The Coward behind the Curtain (1908)
That Master of Ours (1908)
A Royal Indiscretion (1909)
The Interrupted Kiss (1909)
The Girl in the Blue Dress (1909)
The Lovely Mrs Blake (1910)
Live Men's Shoes (1910)
The Twin Sisters (1911)
A Drama of the Telephone (1911)
Violet Forster's Lover (1912)
Sam Briggs: His Book (1912)
Judith Lee: Some Pages from her Life (1912)
The Master of Deception (1913)
Justice—Suspended (1913)
If It Please You (1913)
The Woman in the Car (1914)
Molly's Husband (1914)
Margot—and her Judges (1914)
The Man with Nine Lives (1915)
Love in Fetters (1915)
His Love or his Life (1915)
The Flying Girl (1915)
Violet Forster's Lover (1916)
The Adventures of Judith Lee (1916)
Sam Briggs, V.C. (1916)
Coming of Age (1916)
The Great Temptation (1916)
The Deacon's Daughter (1917)
On the Jury (1918)
Orders to Marry ([1918)
Outwitted (1919)
Apron-Strings (1920)

Periodicals

For Debt, Windsor Magazine (January 1902)
Returning a Verdict, Cornhill Magazine (January 1896)
The Lost Duchess, Cornhill Magazine (January 1895)
Mrs Riddles Daughter, All the Year Round (17 March 1894)
An Episcopal Scandal, Cornhill Magazine (February 1894)
A Rubber or Two, All the Year Round (16 September 1893)
A First Night, Cornhill Magazine (April 1893)
The Mystery of Philip Bennion's Death, Household Words (3/10/17/24/31 December 1892)
The Princess Margaretta, Household Words (3 December 1892)

The Puzzle, Cornhill Magazine (November 1892)
A Victim to Art, All the Year Round (2 July 1892)
The Burglar's Blunder, Derby Mercury (24 June 1891)
Pourquoipas, All the Year Round (9/16 May 1891)
The Pipe, Cornhill Magazine (March 1891)
When Greek Joined Greek, Household Words (6 September 1890)
His First Experiment, Cornhill Magazine (September 1890)
"Mignonette", All the Year Round (9 August 1890)
The Long Arm of Coincidence, Household Words (24 May 1890)
The Match of the Season, Cornhill Magazine (May 1890)
A Set of Chessmen, Cornhill Magazine (April 1890)
A Dream of Diamonds, Household Words (7 December 1889)
My Uncle's Flirtation, Household Words (16 November 1889)
"Em", Household Words (2 November 1889)
The Barnes Mystery: An Adventure of Judith Lee, Strand Magazine (October 1916)
"Scandalous!", Strand Magazine (August 1916)
What Fell on her Hat, Strand Magazine (April 1916)
The Adventures of Sam Briggs: On the Film, Strand Magazine (March 1916)
A Set of Chessmen, Cassell's Magazine of Fiction and Popular Literature (Dec 1915)
Sam Briggs Becomes a Soldier: A Fighting Man, Strand Magazine (December 1915)
Sam Briggs Becomes a Soldier: On the Way Home, Strand Magazine (November 1915)
Sam Briggs Becomes a Soldier: An Official Mistake, Strand Magazine (October 1915)
Sam Briggs Becomes a Soldier: In their Own Gas, Strand Magazine (September 1915)
Sam Briggs Becomes a Soldier: Sanctuary, Strand Magazine (August 1915)
Sam Briggs Becomes a Soldier: In the Nick of Time, Strand Magazine (July 1915)
Sam Briggs Becomes a Soldier: A Night Surprise for the Germans, Strand Magazine (June 1915)
Sam Briggs Becomes a Soldier: In the Trenches, Strand Magazine (May 1915)
Sam Briggs Becomes a Soldier: Baptism of Fire, Strand Magazine (April 1915)
Sam Briggs Becomes a Soldier: Two Stripes, Strand Magazine (March 1915)
Life in the King's New Army: Jack Carpenter's True Story, VI: Career for our Boys, Daily Mail (27 February 1915)
Life in the King's New Army: Jack Carpenter's True Story, V: The Tailor and the Man, Daily Mail (26 February 1915)
Life in the King's New Army: Jack Carpenter's True Story, IV: Hutments', Daily Mail (25 February 1915)
Life in the King's New Army: Jack Carpenter's True Story, III: First-Rate Fighting Men', Daily Mail (24 February 1915)
Life in the King's New Army: Jack Carpenter's True Story, II: The Berwick Borderers, Daily Mail (23 February 1915)
Life in the King's New Army: Jack Carpenter's True Story, I: Crossed Swords, Daily Mail (22 February 1915)
Sam Briggs Becomes a Soldier: A Man in the Making, Strand Magazine (February 1915)
Sam Briggs Becomes a Soldier: Sam Briggs Becomes a Soldier, Strand Magazine (January 1915)
The Amazing Visitor, Strand Magazine (December 1914)
Looping the Loop: An Adventure of Sam Briggs, Strand Magazine (August 1914)
The Torch, Strand Magazine (October 1913)
"Gaiety" Abroad, Strand Magazine (September 1913), 274-82
A Self-Appointed Guardian, English Illustrated Magazine (August 1913)
For the Cause, Strand Magazine (April 1913)

The Adventures of Judith Lee: The Affair of the Montagu Diamonds, Strand Magazine (February 1913)

The Adventures of Judith Lee: Mandragora, Strand Magazine (August 1912)

The Adventures of Judith Lee: "8 Elm Grove—Back Entrance", Strand Magazine (July 1912)

The Adventures of Judith Lee: The Restaurant Napolitain, Strand Magazine (June 1912)

The Adventures of Judith Lee: Uncle Jack, Strand Magazine (May 1912)

The Adventures of Judith Lee: Was It by Chance Only? Strand Magazine (April 1912)

The Adventures of Judith Lee: Isolda, Strand Magazine (March 1912)

The Adventures of Judith Lee: "Auld Lang Syne", Strand Magazine (January 1912)

The Adventures of Judith Lee: The Miracle, Strand Magazine (December 1911)

The Adventures of Judith Lee: Matched

The Burglary in Berkeley Square, Pearson's Magazine (December 1908)

The River of Light, Strand Magazine (December 1908)

The Girl in the Light Blue Dress, Strand Magazine (October 1908)

O'Rourke of the Saucy Sixth, Grand Magazine (June 1908)

The Adventures of Sam Briggs: The Limerick, Strand Magazine (February 1908)

The Adventures of Sam Briggs: The Star of Romance, Strand Magazine (July 1907)

The Adventures of Sam Briggs: A Social Evening, Strand Magazine (April 1907)

My Best Story and Why I Think So No. 21: The Strange Occurrences in Canterstone Gaol, Grand Magazine (October 1906)

The Adventures of Sam Briggs: That Hansom, Strand Magazine (May 1906)

The Adventures of Sam Briggs: Her Fourth, Strand Magazine (December 1905)

The Adventures of Sam Briggs: A Modest Half-Crown, Strand Magazine (November 1905)

The Adventures of Sam Briggs: The Gift Horse, Strand Magazine (March 1905)

My Wedding Day, Strand Magazine (January 1905)

The Adventures of Sam Briggs: The Girl on the Sands, Strand Magazine (October 1904)

The Parson, the Soldier, and the Child, London Magazine (November 1903)

The Girl and the Boy, London Magazine (October 1903)

By Whose Hand? New Short Novel by Richard Marsh, Answers (1 August – 31 October 1903)

A Girl Who Couldn't, Strand Magazine (January 1903)

The Kit-Bag, Windsor Magazine, 17 (January 1903), 298-309

Their Reasons: Two Hitherto Unreported Conversations, House Annual (1902)

At Large: Being the Strange Perils and Experiences of George Otway, Suspect, Answers (12 July - 27 December 1902)

The Handwriting, Strand Magazine (June 1902)

La Haute Finance, Windsor Magazine (March 1902)

A Wonderful Girl, Strand Magazine (March 1902)

Skittles, English Illustrated Magazine, (February/March 1902)

Breaking the Ice, Strand Magazine (February 1902)

My Aunt's Excursion, Windsor Magazine (January 1902)

The Haunted Chair: The Story of a Strange Mystery, Harmsworth London Magazine (January 1902)

Miss Donne's Great Gamble, Strand Magazine (November 1901)

The Man in the Glass Cage; or The Strange Story of the Twickenham Peerage, Manchester Times, (6 September – 27 December 1901

The Adventures of Augustus Short: Things Which I Have Done for Others, and Wish I Hadn't: The Address Which I Gave for Rudman, Cassell's Magazine (November 1901)

The Adventures of Augustus Short: Things Which I Have Done for Others, and Wish I Hadn't: Jones's Love Affair, Cassell's Magazine (October 1901)

The Adventures of Augustus Short: Things Which I Have Done for Others, and Wish I Hadn't: The Duel I Fought of Jarvis, Cassell's Magazine (September 1901)

The Adventures of Augustus Short: Things Which I Have Done for Others, and Wish I Hadn't: Griffin's Offspring, Cassell's Magazine (August 1901)

The Adventures of Augustus Short: Things Which I Have Done for Others, and Wish I Hadn't: McCulloch's Shoes, Cassell's Magazine (July 1901)

The Adventures of Augustus Short: Things Which I Have Done for Others, and Wish I Hadn't: The Fitzroy-Jenkinsons' Rooms, Cassell's Magazine (June 1901)

Staggers, Windsor Magazine (April 1901)

How I Drove a Motor Car for Randal, Strand Magazine (April 1901)

The Disappearance of Mrs Macrecham: The Amazing Story of a Strange Cat, Harmsworth Monthly Pictorial Magazine (March 1901)

The Irregularity of the Juryman, Strand Magazine (December 1900)

The Strange Fortune of Pollie Blythe: The Story of a Chinese "God", Manchester Times (12 October 1900 – 8 February 1901)

Pugh's Poisoned Ring, Harmsworth Monthly Pictorial Magazine (October 1900)

Willyum, Penny Illustrated Paper and Illustrated Times, (26 May 1900)

Willyum, Hampshire Telegraph and Naval Chronicle (26 May 1900)

The Goddess: A Demon, Manchester Times (12 January – 30 March 1900)

The Stolen Treaty, Manchester Times (27 October 1899)

For One Night Only, Answers (8 April 1899)

In Full Cry, Manchester Times (3 March – 9 June 1899)

The Colonel's Cane, Cassell's Magazine (February 1899)

The Burglary at Azalea Villa, Manchester Times, (13 January 1899)

The Burglary at Azalea Villa, Newcastle Weekly Courant (14 January 1899)

Our Christmas Burglar, Answers (17 December 1898)

Something to his Advantage, Manchester Times (7 October – 4 November 1898)

A Lesson in Sculling, Newcastle Weekly Courant (October 1898)

That Five Hundred Pound Price, Harmsworth Monthly Pictorial Magazine (September 1898)

The Chancellor's Ward, Harmsworth Monthly Pictorial Magazine (August 1898)

The Ossington Mystery, Ipswich Journal (1 April – 17 June 1898)

The Duchess of Datchet's Diamonds, New Zealand Graphic and Ladies' Journal (New Zealand) (7 May – 25 June 1898)

The Peril of Paul Lessingham: The Story of a Haunted Man, Answers (13 March – 19 June 1897)

The Purse Which Was Found, Answers (17 April 1897)

The Rector and the Curate, Answers (19 December 1896)

An Illustration of Modern Science, Pall Mall Magazine (November 1896)

A Battlefield Up-to-Date, Idler Magazine (August 1896)

Twins, Idler Magazine (January 1896)

Lady Wishaw's Hand, Leeds Mercury (January 1895)

Young George, St Nicholas (March 1894)

Exchange Is Robbery, Idler Magazine (December 1893 - January 1894)

The Tipster: An Impossible Story, Home Chimes (December 1893)

The Influence of Women, Home Chimes (November 1893)

By Deputy: A Reminiscence of Travel, Home Chimes (October 1893)

Rivals, Home Chimes (September 1893)

Capturing a Convict, Strand Magazine (August 1893)

A Burglar Alarm, Home Chimes (June 1893)

Music Halls and Theatres, Home Chimes (March 1893)

A Strange Bride, Manchester Times (6/13 January 1893)

The Mask, Gentleman's Magazine (December 1892)

A Vision of the Night, Strand Magazine (December 1892)

Nelly, Home Chimes (November 1892)

A Prophet: A Story, New England Magazine (October - November 1892)

Mr Harland's Pupils, Home Chimes (August 1892)

The Brothers in Grey, Home Chimes (April 1892)

The Half-Back, Derby Mercury (March 1892)

The Half-Back, Home Chimes (February 1892)

The Violin, Home Chimes (December 1891)

The Short Story, Home Chimes (August 1891)

Magical Music, Gentleman's Magazine (May 1891)

A Honeymoon Trip, Home Chimes (April 1891)

Mitwaterstraand, Time (September 1890)

A Pack of Cards, Longman's Magazine (August 1890)

The Burglar's Blunder, Ladies' Journal (Canada) (1 July 1890)

The Strange Occurrences in Canterstone Jail, Blackwood's Edinburgh Magazine (June 1890)

A Substitute: The Story of My Last Cricket-Match, Longman's Magazine (June 1890)

The Burglar's Blunder, Gentleman's Magazine (May 1890)

A Silent Witness, Belgravia (October 1889)

A Bed for the Night, Belgravia (Summer 1889)

Payment for a Life, Belgravia (Summer 1888)

www.ingramcontent.com/pod-product-compliance
Lightning Source LLC
Chambersburg PA
CBHW071406170626
46811CB00003B/1277